PRAISE FOR

USA TODAY B[...]

CHRISTIE RIDGWAY

"Emotional and powerful...everything a romance reader could hope for."

--Publishers Weekly (starred review)

"Ridgway's feel-good read, with its perfectly integrated, extremely hot, and well-crafted love scenes, is contemporary romance at its best."

--Booklist (starred review)

"This sexy page-turner [is] a stellar kick-off to Ridgway's latest humor-drenched series."

--Library Journal

"Equally passionate and emotional, this tale will quicken pulses and firmly tug on the heartstrings of readers across the globe. An excellent story that you hope won't ever end!"

--RT Book Reviews (Top Pick)

"Sexy, sassy, funny, and cool, this effervescent sizzler nicely launches Ridgway's new series and is a perfect pick-me-up for a summer's day."

--Library Journal

"Ridgway's latest addition to the Cabin Fever series is heartwarming and gives us hope that second chances are always within reach...This small-town, sweet romance is perfect to remind one that love almost always endures the test of time."

--RT Book Reviews

Also By Christie Ridgway

Also Available

7 Brides for 7 Soldiers

ZANE

7 Brides for 7 Soldiers, #3

CHRISTIE RIDGWAY

Chapter 1

The sound of his name jerked Zane Tucker from his contemplation of the view of the Snake River outside the diner windows. His foot kicked out, catching the legs of the empty chair across from him and sending it crashing to the floor. "Hell," he muttered, clambering to his size fourteen feet to right the thing, even as he glared at the intruder into his little private reverie.

"What do you want?" he demanded of the buzz-haired guy.

"Touchy, touchy," the other man said.

He looked familiar to Zane, but just about everyone looked familiar in his small hometown of Eagle's Ridge, Washington, situated near the Blue Mountains. With only ten thousand total residents and a single high school, the thirtyish man standing beside his table, wearing an annoying smirk, had to be someone with whom he'd grown up.

Oh, yeah, he thought, a name popping from his memory. Smerkman. Andy Smerkman.

"What's up, Andy?" Zane said, dropping back into his seat. He tried to sound pleasant. He was a friendly, easygoing sort of man. Everybody said so, and it was a prerequisite in dealing with the clients of the adventure watersports business he ran with his twin brother. "Haven't seen you in a while."

"On a visit to the olds," the guy said. "You know, my parents. Stopped in here at No Man's Land for a coffee before heading back to Seattle."

Andy Smerkman, he of the visit to the "olds"—who the hell said that?—was clearly angling for an invitation to join Zane at his table.

If memory served, Andy had always been a lousy fisherman.

"Have a good one," Zane said, picking up his own mug of brew and hoping Smerkman would catch the hint and go away.

Instead he scraped out the chair on the other side of the rectangular wooden table and slid into it. "I heard your brother found himself a lady and it looks permanent."

Zane grunted. Still a surprise, but it was true. The only thing Adam had ever taken seriously was work—first as a rescue swimmer with the Coast Guard, and then later with refurbishing their old boathouse as a youth adventure camp for at-risk kids. But when his Jane had showed up at A To Z Watersports, Adam's legendary focus had widened.

"I heard your sister lassoed the town golden boy, Ryder Westbrook."

Bristling, Zane sent out another glare. Like all big brothers, he felt protective of his little sister, Bailey. "*He* was lucky to catch *her* eye." And Bailey seemed so happy that even though the Tuckers had been feuding with the Westbrooks for years upon years, Zane could only be pleased for her. She'd been put through the wringer by some NYC asshole, but she'd come home and found the best man for her.

"And I've also heard that you've been moping around town ever since your sister and your brother found true love."

What? Outrage filled Zane's chest, hardening his muscles to cement. "Moping?" he growled out.

"Uh-huh," Smerkman said, looking up as Brenda Morgan, who ran the diner alongside Zane's dad, bustled near with a steaming carafe of coffee. She filled the waiting empty mug then topped off Zane's.

Smerkman smirked again. "Word is you're walking around looking all lonesome since you're now the babe-less Tucker twin. The only Tucker sibling without a soulmate."

Don't punch the guy, Zane commanded himself, even as his fingers curled into fists. He was a friendly, cheerful, easy-going sort. Everybody said so. But everybody now was saying he was looking lonesome? And worse, perhaps *pitying* him?

Brenda slanted Zane a sympathetic look. Damn it! Did she feel sorry for his babe-less self too or was it mere sympathy for having to share space with the dim-witted Smerkman?

The bells on the diner door caught Zane's attention. A pair of men entered, and he lurched to his feet, setting the mugs on the table rattling. Patrons looked over in some alarm, but he was accustomed to that. Zane was a big man at six-four, two-twenty, and he tended to boom and clatter his way through life.

Though he didn't try to frighten little kids or overwhelm fragile women, it just happened that way.

He was athletic on and in the water—a true riverman to his marrow—and actually adept on mountain trails too.

It was only being indoors that gave him trouble. Probably because of the early years of inactivity that severe childhood asthma had forced upon him. Now grown and grown out of the condition, walls and roofs could no longer contain him comfortably.

"Where are you going?" Smerkman said, as Zane headed toward the newcomers taking stools at the counter.

Away from your recap of local gossip. Any more comments on the alleged state of his psyche and he'd be in danger of taking a swing at that annoying face and its irksome smirk. "Gotta see a guy about a bet."

His rugged rubber soles sounded loud on the scarred wooden floor as he paced toward the newcomers. They swiveled around as he came to a stop behind them. "Wyatt," he said, nodding at the man on the left. Then he fished for his phone and brought up a photo. He brandished it in the face of the guy on the right. "Look here, Denver."

Denver—his name was actually Mike, but he went by the place he'd hailed from, before he came to the Eagle's Ridge area to work at a dude ranch— groaned, loud and long. He was around twenty-two, a decade younger than Zane. "You didn't really do it, did you?"

"Proof is in the picture, buddy." He turned the phone so Wyatt Chandler could have a look too. "Dressed up that statue of town founder John Westbrook at one end of Sentinel Bridge. In broad daylight, as stipulated, and I didn't get caught, also as stipulated." Zane didn't add that he'd released the leash on his dog who then provided a helpful distraction by galloping through the nearby park, chasing squirrels, knocking over trash cans, and wreaking other general but benign mayhem.

Wyatt shook his head. "Nothing stops Insane Zane."

A nickname he'd been given all those years ago during a semester of high school detention, in honor of the crazy bets he was in the habit of making. "Don't you think the statue looks good in that spangly Wonder Woman outfit? I thought the headband was a nice touch. Who knew you could find a male size XXL costume? But the Internet has everything."

Looking as if he was fighting a smile, Wyatt shook his head again. "I thought the quarrel between the Tuckers and the Westbrooks had simmered down now. Aren't you afraid something like that will start it up again if people find out the statue-defiling perp was you?"

"Nah. Not a chance. Not with Ryder and Bailey our own happy-ever-after Romeo and Juliet."

"About that..." Wyatt hesitated. "You doing okay?"

Zane narrowed his eyes. "I'm doing great."

Smerkman, who now stood at Zane's elbow, had the balls to put in his two cents. "Moping," he declared. "Heard it from my mom who heard it from my aunt—"

"Take off the boots," Zane said over him in a steely voice, his gaze on the fancy cowboy pair on Denver's feet. Anything to deflect the conversation and his renewed desire to punch a wall—or at least Smerkman's nose.

Maybe he'd been a bit out-of-step lately,

especially since Adam had coupled up with Jane. It was…odd, a life change, to have both siblings now pledged to romantic partners. Perhaps he'd experienced a little loneliness in recent days too, but by God, he wasn't moping in a way that anyone should be noticing.

He had more pride than that.

"Zane." Denver glanced down at his fancy footwear. "I really can't see why you'd want them. You're more of the hiking boots type."

"You'd not be entirely right," Wyatt told the other man. "You're talking to a former Army Cavalry Scout."

Denver's eyes went wide. Yeah, it had been a surprise to Zane's family too. Not that he'd opted for military service, that was a familiar route for the young people of Eagle's Ridge which had been founded by veterans of World War II. But despite all his ease on the water, he didn't go Coast Guard like his twin or aim to become a SEAL like Wyatt.

"I was a kid," he said, shrugging. One who had watched hundreds of hours of old Westerns when he'd been cooped up inside the house until he was fourteen. "There's spurs. And a Stetson. Look it up."

Denver blinked. "You rode a horse?"

"No. Recon specialist. Until I tore up my shoulder and came home after ten years in. But enough stalling." He sent a pointed look at the boots. "Hope your socks don't have holes in them."

The kid from Colorado took his time taking off the tooled leather, but Zane remained unmoved. "That should teach you not to make bets when you've had a beer too many."

"That should teach you to never make a bet with

Zane," Wyatt said.

Zane turned to his old friend, another of the West Side kids who'd grown up on the "wrong" side of the river, just like him. Wyatt had spent years as a SEAL but then arrived in town a couple of weeks ago, fresh out of the Navy. "How are you settling in to civilian life?"

Wyatt shrugged. "Okay."

Which said nothing at all. "Have you considered your next move?"

"A job, you mean?" Wyatt shrugged again. "Something will come up."

Zane eyed the other man's fit form and the bouncing knee that proclaimed he was used to doing and not dithering. He could relate. "Maybe we could find you something on the water—"

"I'm not up for that," Wyatt said quickly, then cleared his throat. "I've had some other offers. Right now I'm just spending time with Gran. She's getting on, you know."

His grandmother had raised him after his parents died. But Wyatt talked about the older woman as if she was a doddering elderly, not the vital senior citizen that Zane knew to be active in her church's social club and other endeavors around town. As Denver handed him the boots, Zane took them in hand while studying Wyatt's closed expression.

Something was up.

"I don't know that your granny requires a round-the-clock caretaker," he said. "She's getting about just fine, I've seen her myself."

"She needs me," Wyatt said stubbornly.

"Maybe some of the time," Zane conceded, glancing again at the man's bouncing knee and then at his steely jaw. This guy needed to lighten up. "But you have some free hours for a gig as a rodeo clown, don't you? I have a contact. The job promises plenty of action, danger, and the weird face paint too. As a matter of fact, I bet—"

"I'm good, Zane," Wyatt said sharply, too sharply, without even a hint of a smile. Then he ran a hand through his hair. "Sorry about that. Coming back home...it's made me a little edgy, I guess."

"I'm glad I got out of this town," Smerkman declared. "Because it's made Wyatt edgy and Zane's moping—"

"I'm *not* moping!" Hell, that didn't sound pleasant or friendly or the least bit calm. Zane could feel every customer in the diner staring at him, and guessed if he looked that their gazes would be filled with pity. The need to knock something down rose inside him and he sucked in a breath to push it back. "You know what? I gotta go."

Fully aware of the stares from every corner of the room, he made his way to the rear of the restaurant. Was this how it was going to be? Slowly smothered in sympathy by those around him because he was the un-partnered Tucker?

Since when had he shown any inclination to secure a missus anyway?

Never.

A long time ago he'd come to the realization that a woman looking for a long-term man would want one with less hard muscle and more softness inside. Less raw power and more gentle romance. That was not him.

He bypassed the kitchen where Brenda and his dad were taking a quick breather between the breakfast and lunch rush. His dog, Gambler, waited in the storeroom, where a full water dish and a cushioned bed were always available for his visits.

The yellow Lab jumped to his feet when Zane opened the door, rushing to greet him as if they'd been parted for months instead of less than an hour. Going down on one knee, he set aside the cowboy boots and rubbed his hands over the dog's warm and wiggling body. Gambler's sweeping tail knocked a plastic-wrapped stack of paper napkins off a shelf and when Zane reached over to retrieve it, his own elbow tumbled a second stack.

Chuckling, he put both back into place, then clipped the dog's leash onto his collar. "We'll always have each other, won't we, boy? Birds of a feather."

As he led the dog toward the rear door, Brenda wandered out of the kitchen. "Leaving already? You didn't have more than coffee."

"I'm good, thanks, Bren." The concerned kindness on her face and in her green eyes made him hunch his shoulders. After their mother took off for the bright lights of Hollywood, she'd been a warm presence for all the Tucker siblings, but right now he thought she might be about to offer him some of that unwelcome concern for his babe-less—as Smerkman had put it—state.

Tugging on Gambler's leash, he edged closer to the door. "I'll see you later."

"You know," she said, "it's okay if you feel a bit out of sorts. Anyone would feel a little lost with this new shift in the family dynamics."

Out of sorts? Lost? Frustration, embarrassment, and exasperation roiled in his belly. Did he really seem so doleful? "Brenda—"

"Maybe if I fixed you up with someone," she continued, in a voice soft with compassion. "There's a woman in my photography class who has a daughter…"

That was it. *It.* He drew the line when sympathy turned to talk of fix-ups. To escape a renewed urge to knock something over, Zane managed to force out some non-committal noise and shoved open the door.

Apparently energized by the fresh air and his owner's distraction, Gambler took a sudden leap, the leash yanking from Zane's loosened hold. The dog took off, splashing through the rain puddles in the parking area in the direction of the front entrance. Zane followed, cursing the animal, himself, and the whole world.

Maybe he did deserve to be pitied.

Then, in horror, he watched as Gambler did exactly what his master had been itching to do. The dog knocked something over.

Someone.

And the person who truly warranted a hefty dose of pity was a delicate-looking woman with dark blonde hair who now lay flat on her back on the sidewalk, books, purse, and various personal belongings scattered around her.

Harper Grace stared up at the blue sky, her heart in her throat, her breath backed up in her lungs. There was a ringing in her ears. *What just happened?*

Then a slavering monster entered her field of vision, hairy and toothy and totally terrifying. She choked out a sound and tried scrambling backward, using her heels and her shoulders. Sitting up would only put her closer to the beast.

The sound of a deep voice penetrated her hearing. "Gambler! For God's sake! *Gambler!*" The furry thing was hauled back to be replaced by something even bigger who now took his own turn to stare down at her from the most startling aquamarine-colored eyes she'd ever seen.

"Are you all right, miss?" the creature asked, a man creature, obviously, in a denim work shirt and jeans.

Some instinct caused her to make another feeble attempt at a rear scramble.

He frowned. "Do you need medical assistance?"

Her head was dizzy and her mouth was dry but her limbs appeared to be working and nothing seemed to be broken on the inside either. At the sound of an insistent jingle, she glanced over and saw the original monster sitting on its haunches, looking at her like she might be raw meat.

She swallowed. "You have a good grip on that...that thing?" she asked, noting the leash in the big man's hand was connected to a collar of thick metal links around the beast's neck.

"He's Gambler," the man replied. "My ill-mannered dog. And we're both very sorry he toppled you."

Her side-eye glance at the canine didn't convince her he felt the least bit apologetic. Not with his pink tongue hanging out like that.

"Damn." The man's eyes narrowed, and he hunkered down, his long legs folding in half. "You're really scared."

"No." She denied the charge as she took in his tree trunk-sized thighs. "I was just...startled."

Not scared. Because she'd moved to Eagle's

Ridge to be someone different. To try different things. To shed the "boring" that her ex said he'd tired of. The Harper Grace who'd been nervous around big dogs and reluctant to experience a bunch of other things had been left behind in San Francisco.

"Let me help you up," the man said, holding out his free hand. His palm looked to be as big as a dinner plate.

"I can do it." Half-rolling, she got to her knees and then to her feet. Still with one cautious eye on the dog, she tugged at the hem of her long black cardigan, brushed at the leaves clinging to her black pants, then paused, noting the two massive dirty paw prints on her formerly pristine white shirt.

"You can send me the cleaning bill for your clothes," Gambler's owner said.

"Nonsense." Harper was proud of the brisk tone of her voice. "It's nothing a little laundry detergent can't handle." But she'd have to return to her condo for different clothes before visiting any more of the Eagle's Ridge businesses. If she was going to ask to leave flyers and post notices about her upcoming charity event to benefit the library, she figured the new librarian should appear tidy and clean.

The man stretched out a long arm and snagged her fallen purse. The contents had spilled out on the sidewalk and he plucked up those too, tossing pen, pencil, wallet, and ChapStick inside. Then he straightened to his full height and handed over the black leather bag.

"Thank you." She settled the strap on her shoulder and then reached for the plastic portfolio he held out next. It had come from the copy shop just that morning and she was glad that the papers inside hadn't been scattered. With the cement still damp from an earlier rain, she'd have had a sodden mess on her hands.

"I'm really sorry," the man said again, and turned to glare at the dog. "We plan to take obedience classes as soon as he overcomes some of his fears. Right now I think it would put too much stress on him."

Curiosity got the better of her. "He has...fears?" And suffered from stress? The dog looked big enough to intimidate anyone and anything.

Gambler's owner nodded, his expression serious. "Skateboards. Doorbells. Bubble wrap. Don't get me started on frogs."

A gurgle of laughter worked its way up Harper's throat. "Bubble wrap? *Frogs?*" She shifted her gaze to the dog again, and suddenly he seemed much less menacing. "Poor guy."

"You say that because you've forgotten the mud he's transferred to your clothes." Then the man's gaze snagged on something nearby and he brightened. "Hey, maybe this will help." Bending again, he scooped up a last refugee from her purse, an instant stain remover stick that she never left home without.

Popping off the top, he took a step forward. "Hold still and I'll..." He froze, his hand hovering a few inches from the smears of dirt on her shirt.

Harper glanced down, saw that a couple of buttons had unfastened, and now the fabric gaped over her breasts, exposing the top inches encased in a pale pink lace bra. "Oh!" Heat rushed from the edge of the intimate garment to the top of her head.

Harper Grace didn't flash strange men in the street!

Her hand flew to the placket, just as a truck

pulled up alongside them. The passenger window rolled down, revealing a familiar female face. Not long ago the woman had come to the library and introduced herself as Jadyn McAllister, an assumed name she'd used because of her unwitting mix-up in a revenge plot on a drug lord. Once the dangerous mess had cleared, she'd returned to the library and explained she was really Jane McAllen.

"Hey, Harper!" she called now. "Is everything okay?"

It would be, as long as no one noticed her fumbling with her shirt buttons and didn't guess she'd been standing partially disrobed on the streets of Eagle's Ridge. "Just fine. How are you?"

The other woman popped her door and then climbed out of the vehicle, just as a man emerged from the driver's side. Harper recognized those blue eyes, the exact same, startling shade as those of Gambler's owner.

He was big like him too, though maybe a bit shorter and leaner, and with similar bone structure to his handsome face.

Because yes, the dog's owner was very handsome, in a very virile, very rugged kind of way. Both men had the kind of masculine good looks that had always unsettled Harper.

"Have you met Adam Tucker?" Jane was asking now, slipping her hand into the crook of the newcomer's elbow.

Children of the mansions in Nob Hill had manners instilled in them at the cradle. Ignoring her usual twinge of stranger-shyness, she held out her hand. "Harper Grace, new county librarian."

His fingers closed over hers for a brief shake, and

then he glanced over at the other man. "I'm guessing you've met my twin."

Ah. That explained the resemblance. "No, not really. We just now—"

"Gambler took her out like a bowling pin," Adam's brother said, grimacing. "We didn't get to introductions yet."

Jane shook her head. "Oh, my. Are you all right, Harper?"

"Just embarrassed."

"Well, you shouldn't be," Jane said. "Zane should have better control of him."

Harper glanced over at the dog's owner. "Zane." Then back at the woman. "Jane."

"I keep telling her she picked the wrong twin," the taller man said with a smile. He had very nice, very white teeth. "What couldn't a power couple named Zane and Jane achieve?"

"More like Tarzan and Jane," his brother muttered, then hitched his lady closer to him.

Harper liked the way Jane leaned into Adam's body in return, trusting and warm, as if she knew she could count on him. As if she knew that he wouldn't be the kind of man to break a two-year engagement on the day she booked the wedding chapel.

She also liked the teasing byplay between the brothers. Her only sibling was a thrill-seeking older sister and though she hadn't been around males much growing up or as an adult, she recognized the approving expression on Zane's face as he watched his brother hug Jane.

"I should get going," Harper ventured now, recalling her need to return home for a clean outfit.

"Or come in the diner and join us for a late

breakfast or an early lunch," Jane said, gesturing to the front door.

"Oh, I couldn't. Not with soiled clothes."

"Dad won't mind," Adam put in. "He owns No Man's Land—the diner—by the way. Sam Tucker."

"I was going to ask him if I could put a poster about the library charity event in the front window," Harper confessed. "But I'll come back later."

"Give it to us," Jane said. "We'll take care of it."

Pleased, Harper began to open the flap on the portfolio. "That would be great." She withdrew one of the 11 x 13-inch tagboard notices. Then Zane was there taking it from her hand.

His eyebrows rose as he read aloud the bold-faced heading. "Get Dirty for Books."

She ignored the ridiculous heat rising on her face. "It was my predecessor's idea. She had most of the logistics in place before her husband was quickly deployed and they had to move across the country. It's a charity mud run. The proceeds will go toward new books."

A grin broke over the big man's face. "I like that. Get dirty." He glanced from the poster to Harper. "Are you going to participate?"

She lifted her chin, not even thinking before she replied, "Of course."

Now why the heck had she said that? she wondered, wanting to slap the heel of her hand to her forehead. She'd had no intention of actually participating in the event, especially as her exercise of choice in San Francisco had been nothing more vigorous than the spin class described as a "beach cruise."

It was Zane Tucker's fault.

He was too handsome and too virile—that must be it.

A guy that good-looking touched a deep, feminine part of her. It would be the same for any woman, she told herself. Looking into those fascinating eyes could compel a female to want unwise things. To make crazy claims. To participate in mud runs!

Still, how could she have actually said so?

Yes, Harper wanted to be different, but not *that* different.

"Really?" the man said now, his gaze sweeping over her body as if assessing her readiness. No doubt he could tell that the only truly fit muscles in her body were the ones used to lift books and turn pages. He looked down at the poster he still held and then back at her face. "You're going to run through four miles of mud and obstacles?"

She felt her chin lift again. "Yes." Oh, God. Oh, *God*. Who had taken over her voice? But with Zane, his brother, Jane, and that dog all looking on, Harper found she couldn't renege now. With a vigorous nod, she doubled-down. "I'm sure I'll find it great fun."

Before she could promise she'd be climbing Everest next, she tucked her purse closer to her body. "Now, if you'll excuse me…"

Goodbyes were quickly said and Jane took the poster, promising to personally ensure it had prominent placement in the diner. Then, with a last wave, Harper headed in the direction of her small condo complex.

Only to find herself accompanied by Zane and the dog.

"Oh," she said, feeling the pinch of a slight frown

between her brows. "Are you going in this direction too?"

"I was planning on it. I take Gambler on walks around town so he can experience different sights and sounds. I'm hoping to desensitize him to his fears."

The dog didn't look that anxious to her at the moment, trotting along with his tongue hanging out, but what did she know?

"We can walk behind you if that would make you more comfortable," Zane offered.

"I don't think I want Gambler where I can't see him."

The man gave another of his grins and she looked away in case it caused blindness. "How did the dog get to be so fearful anyway?" she asked.

"I don't really know. A guy came through town, part of a group of hunters that we get up here. One night at a local bar, he was complaining that the Lab he bought as a hunting dog was no good. He was thinking of dropping it off at an animal shelter on his way back home to Colorado."

"Oh." Harper sent a sympathetic glance to the dog, who was lifting his leg and peeing on a bush, apparently unaware of his close call. "Poor boy."

"I was actually concerned that what the man really intended to do was leave the dog behind at their campsite."

Harper swallowed the sudden lump in her throat. "That's horrible."

"It happens." Zane's mouth flattened. "So I offered to take him off his hands, but the minute I expressed an interest, Mr. Shoot 'Em Up wanted me to pay him three thousand dollars."

"For a dog he was intending to get rid of one way

or another?" Harper frowned. "Did you pay?"

"I enticed him into a bet. If I could get the phone number of a woman in the bar—any woman of his choosing—in less than thirty seconds, then the dog was mine for free. If she refused, then I'd pay him the asking price—"

"And still get the dog."

He smiled. "And still get the dog."

When he didn't continue, she sent him a pointed look. "Well? Obviously I know you got Gambler, but how?"

"Mr. Heartless-and-Smug pointed to a very beautiful woman a few tables over, dressed in stylish city clothes and wearing high-heeled boots that probably cost as much as he wanted to charge me for the animal. Likely the hunter supposed the sophisticated lady would never respond to a come-on from an oversized mountain bumpkin like me."

"But she did," Harper said, certain.

The slyest of grins broke over Zane's face. "Lady Luck was looking out for me that night. The woman in question—an attorney on a visit from LA—just happened to be my high school prom date."

Delighted, she laughed. Then looking around, realized they'd reached the pathway leading to her complex. She halted.

"Congratulations on your good fortune," she told Zane, "though I'm sure any woman in the room would have been just as eager to hand over her contact info—former prom date or no."

"Yeah?" Zane angled his head and the sunlight that took that moment to break through the clouds seemed to catch in his bright, blue-green eyes. "How about you?"

Instantly flustered, Harper hugged her plastic portfolio to her chest. "Men don't customarily ask for my number."

"Is that right?" He didn't look away from her face. "Well, you're in Eagle's Ridge now, where men have eyes and brains—so expect that to change."

The comment left her speechless. For a moment she just stood in dumbfounded silence, but then manners came to her rescue and she stretched out her hand. "I've got to go. Goodbye, Zane Tucker."

"Goodbye, Harper Grace." His big hand enfolded hers.

Sensation shimmied up her arm, a prickly heat that burst across her skin. Her nerve endings danced beneath the surface and she felt as if she'd been tumbled once more, except she was still on her feet.

And Zane's hand continued to hold hers.

Under the influence of that firm clasp, the sky was brighter and the sun was warmer and the trees were taller than any she'd ever seen before in her life.

It was like a new world.

Her pulse started racing.

"You're in Eagle's Ridge now," Zane repeated, a low murmur.

Eagle's Ridge, where he'd said she should expect things to change.

But this didn't feel like simple change to her, she thought, as worry chased a shiver running down her spine. This felt like a sudden, brilliant, not-just-a-little-bit scary revolution, and Harper was worried that even a woman determined to make over her life wouldn't be able to handle it.

Chapter 2

Strolling into No Man's Land, Zane saw Wyatt seated at the counter and took the stool beside him. The other man grunted in greeting, without taking his gaze off the fragrant bowl of chili placed in front of him.

"Long day?" Zane inquired, gesturing to the waitress to bring him his own helping of beans and beef. "I spent the morning teaching a kayaking class that we're offering through the community college, the lunch hour sending emails confirming reservations that came through our website, and this afternoon Adam and I each led a raft of kids from a charter school in Utah through our easiest rapids."

He was pleasantly tired and more than happy about how the high season for the business was shaping up. His adventure watersports company, an idea he'd hit upon after getting out of the service and spending hours rehabbing his damaged shoulder with an oar on the water, had started small but had grown exponentially when Adam joined him two years earlier.

Zane glanced over at the man on the neighboring stool who continued to methodically spoon food into his mouth. "What about you, Wyatt?"

"I drove Gran to the grocery store," Wyatt said, his glum tone signaling he'd found it less than fulfilling.

A bowl and paper-wrapped utensils were set in front of Zane. "You need to start hitting the gym, man."

"Five a.m. I'm there every day."

"Then come over to our place afterward and I'll fix you up with a kayak. Time on the water will soothe the restless beast."

"Gran wants me to spend my days gluing her hundreds of photos into her dozens of blank albums," Wyatt said, crumbling more crackers into his bowl. "Or she has a crony with an idea for a startup...I could be a private driver chauffeuring seniors to the local casinos and back."

"In case they get drunk on the penny slot machines?"

"You don't think that job sounds like uber-fun?"

Zane grinned as he dug into his own chili. "At least you haven't completely lost your sense of humor."

They ate in companionable silence for a few minutes until a tickle skittered across the back of Zane's neck. He glanced around, his gaze homing in on a figure just settling into a chair at a two-top in a corner of the diner. It had been a few days since his dog had collided with the pretty new librarian named Harper Grace. As he watched, she pulled a paperback out of her purse and opened it to the place held by a bookmark.

"What are you looking at?" his neighbor said, craning his neck to peer over his shoulder. "Oh, baby," Wyatt continued, with distinct admiration. "You know, she only gets better and better."

Zane's head whipped around. "What?" he asked, staring at the other man. "You know her?"

"Miss Woody? Hello? The one whose porch you recently decorated with rose petals? Just the object of our teenage lust when she ran detention hall that semester we had it in high school. Made the suffering *so* much easier."

Following Wyatt's gaze, Zane relaxed. It was indeed Diana Woods, aka "Miss Woody" who had attracted his friend's attention. She'd been a hot teacher in her mid-twenties when she'd supervised the pair of them as well as a bunch of other guys during their very own version of *The Breakfast Club*. Today, she was still hot, still a busty redhead who must be near forty.

"So she really never married?" Wyatt asked.

"Nope."

"Hmm." Wyatt turned back to his food. "Maybe she's lonely?"

Lonely. The word sent Zane's gaze back to the young woman in the corner of the room, who smiled her thanks as Mandy the new waitress slid a pot of tea and a cup and saucer in front of her. Then she returned to her book.

"If you're looking for female companionship," he said, elbowing his neighbor, "you should strike up a conversation with the woman over there."

"Where?" Wyatt half-swiveled on his chair.

"Who?"

"The light-haired female in the brown sweater. With the book."

Wyatt took another moment. "Oh, I see. She sort of blends into the wall."

Zane frowned. "She does not."

Wyatt shrugged.

"She's new in town. Took the place of the former county librarian. You're new back in town—seems fitting you go over to her table and welcome her to the community or something."

His friend's brows rose. "What's this all about?"

Harper Grace was sitting by herself. That didn't seem right. A delicate, pretty creature such as herself shouldn't be alone in that secluded corner. "I met her the other day. Well, Gambler knocked her over and I had to issue an apology. She seems nice."

Wyatt grunted.

Zane tried again. "Two single people. You never know what might happen."

"At the moment I don't need a woman in my life," Wyatt said. "Why don't you go talk to her?"

Because, when the two of them stood in front of her condo building, she'd run from him like he was a starving Sasquatch and she was a sweet-smelling light snack. Because she wasn't his type, no way, no how. He had an instinct about these things—more like the result of lessons learned—and he wasn't going to make move one on a woman who was looking for flowers and forever when everyone knew he was rowdy fun and right nows.

Zane checked her out again. Now she was picking at a garden salad. Was that all she was planning to eat for dinner?

"Geez, Z." Wyatt snorted. "Go talk to the woman. You know you want to. And then people around here will start talking about that, instead going on and on about your long face and sad eyes."

Hell. "That hasn't died down?" *The babe-less Tucker twin. The only Tucker sibling without a soulmate.* Though he was happy for his sibs, it was starting to sink in, more and more by the day, that this change would take some getting used to.

"Nope. Still lots of gossip about you being lonesome."

Irritation crawled up Zane's spine. "I gotta go," he said, deciding to escape the feeling by heading home and doing something constructive like a thousand Spiderman pushups until he cared about nothing but pouring a gallon of water down his throat. Leaving cash by his unfinished bowl, he started to stalk out, then changed his mind and opted to do the decent thing first and say goodbye to his dad.

Maybe a little Pop-chat would even his keel, actually. His father, Sam Tucker, was a laid-back guy, who'd for the most part coolly handled his wife leaving him, his kids, and Eagle's Ridge for her Hollywood dreams years before. He'd just continued on continuing on, content with running the diner and now enjoying having his grown kids back in the area.

Zane swung into the kitchen to find his laid-back father glaring at his right-hand woman, Brenda Morgan. Both stood, arms akimbo, facing off at the rear of the space while burgers sizzled unattended on the grill. "You're going to make me crazy, you know that?" Sam demanded.

"This isn't about you," Brenda hissed, clearly as angry.

Oh-kay. Unsure what to do besides the obvious, Zane headed for the meat and tended to it with an efficiency born of years of helping out. When he was a little kid, he'd envied the time his brother and sister spent in the diner's kitchen with their dad. His mom had worried the smoke might exacerbate his asthma and he'd been banned from the premises. But then he'd gotten well and she'd gotten sick of being mom and wife.

In high school, when he wasn't playing or practicing sports, he'd sat in the diner doing his homework, rising when needed to plate up a meal or deliver it to a patron.

"It's dangerous," Zane's dad said now, eyes still narrowed. "How am I supposed to sleep at night?"

"I'm meeting a man for a drink, Sam," Brenda said. "Not inviting a serial killer home for a sleepover."

Okay, just the thought of Brenda out with some stranger gave Zane pause too. She was mid-fifties and trim, with her long dark hair in its usual waist-length braid. After their mother left, she'd always been there for the Tucker family. It made him protective of her.

Clearly the idea of Brenda getting hurt in any way got under his dad's skin too.

Bailey had been making noises about a possible romance kindling between Sam and Brenda. Adam didn't agree and it seemed unlikely to Zane as well. Brenda had been a manager here for years and years and a widow for ten, after her Marine husband had been killed in action. Wouldn't something have already happened if something was going to happen? His dad had never shown much interest or put much effort into changing his single status.

"Maybe I'll join this online service too," Sam now said, making a liar out of his younger son.

"You'll have to check under Personality that you're grouchy and unreasonable," Brenda countered. "Good luck finding somebody who wants to take that on."

Then she swept past his dad, pausing only when she caught sight of Zane. "Oh, hi, honey," she said, patting him on the arm. "How are you?"

Baffled by the scene he'd just witnessed, Zane trailed her out of the kitchen and into the diner. There, his gaze slid straight to Harper Grace again, still solo, still reading while poking at those boring greens.

"Brenda," he said.

Slowing her steps, the older woman glanced back. "Yes?"

"Could you, uh, maybe take a few minutes and talk to the woman in the corner?"

Frowning, Brenda shifted her gaze. "Is there a problem with her order?"

I have a problem with seeing her sitting all by herself. "No, it's not that. It's just…never mind."

"All right then." The older woman strode for the door, looking back toward the kitchen as she neared the exit.

Zane did the same, to see his father staring out the pass-through, his expression not the least bit laid-back.

Yeah, time for his son to escape the confusion of that, too. Time to go home.

But while his mind had every intention of taking himself to his A-frame cabin in the woods, it was his feet that instead moved in the direction of the quiet customer in the corner.

For some inexplicable reason, she pulled at him.

He told himself he had legitimate excuses to take a minute to chat. She was having a meal at the family business—making sure it was up to par made sense. And then there was her relationship status. Maybe she wasn't single after all, so his encouraging Wyatt to chat her up had been needless.

But if she didn't come as a pair, then he could do something about these solo meals. Eagle's Ridge was a small town and he knew every eligible bachelor in the vicinity. While anyone acquainted with him might scoff at Zane playing matchmaker, well, perhaps it could become his new hobby, like Brenda's photography.

First, though, he had to put her at ease.

Evidence suggested—that evidence being how she'd run from him following their goodbye outside her condo—he more than made the woman skittish.

With that thought on the forefront of his mind, he moved through the tables as deftly as possible, only once knocking a knife off a table. The plastic kiddie glass that tumbled to the floor couldn't be blamed entirely on him. When he'd walked past a high chair he'd tried smiling at the toddler perched in it. The kid had let out a shriek of tiny terror and his flailing hand had released the teddy bear-emblazoned cup.

Sigh. He didn't *try* to frighten little kids. He didn't *want* to overwhelm fragile women.

The particular fragile woman he was heading for didn't sense his approach. Her head remained bent over her book and he considered calling out her name, as soft as can be, when his big foot bashed one of her table's legs. The entire thing jumped, rattling plate and utensils.

Harper's head jerked up and so did her hand, sending her book on a header into her lap. The scrap of fabric holding her place flew, fluttering to the wooden floor to land beside his round-toed hiking boots.

Zane grimaced. "Sorry to startle you," he said, bending to retrieve the fallen bookmark.

She swallowed, her pretty gray eyes now glued to his face, her fingertips pressed to her throat. "That's all right, Mr. Tucker. Is there…is there something I can do for you?"

"Call me Zane." He tried on a smile. "Mr. Tucker is my grandpa or my dad."

A small nod. "Yes. Zane."

They stared at each other another long moment and only a fool could remain unaware of the sizzling awareness arcing in the air between them.

Okay, he'd noticed it the other day, too, but thought perhaps it was a one-off.

Because he shouldn't be attracted to her, he knew that. But just looking at the line of her delicate jaw and the sweet softness of her unpainted mouth made his dick hard.

There. His thoughts were uncouth and raw and she'd probably run screaming if he ever confessed he'd spent one entire night recalling that brief glimpse of her small breasts in pale pink lace.

Glancing down, he noted the bookmark in his hand. "What's this?" he asked, studying the tiny even stitches that created the iconic design of a famous bridge. "The Golden Gate?"

"I'm from San Francisco," she said.

"You're a city girl."

"Mmm-hmm." She nodded. "And that's petit

point—it's a type of needlework. My grandmother taught me how to do it."

"You made this?" he asked. Of course she did. It was as pretty and tidy as the rest of her.

She nodded again.

"It's very nice." He continued to hold it in his hand, his thumb lightly brushing the surface as he wondered what to say next. Something about the weather. Or a remark about her salad. Stick to the innocuous and impersonal, he told himself. *Don't scare her off in any way.*

"Are you seeing someone?" he blurted out. Good God. Could he get any clumsier? What the hell was *wrong* with him?

She glanced down, licked her lips, then lifted her gaze to meet his. "Are you asking me out?"

"I…uh…" Was he? Well, no. Despite his attraction to her, his question had to do with that matchmaking hobby he was currently considering. There were guys in town who would treat her right and with whom she could find what she wanted. Flowers and forever. More than what he had to offer—which could only be categorized as shallow and short-term.

But…

What would it hurt if they did go out? It might not be so bad. As a matter of fact, one tame little date might actually squelch his inconvenient interest in her altogether.

He opened his mouth to suggest dinner and a movie, telling himself for one night he could use his inside voice and play gentleman through a few courses and a rom com. Then something caught his eye.

Teenagers, a group of four boys, finishing up their meals of burgers and shakes at a table by the door. They were giving each other looks that Zane recognized all too well. The shifty expressions on their faces and the tense lines of their skinny frames boded ill for Dad's cash register and Mandy's tip jar.

Because once upon a time—on a bet, naturally—Zane had attempted the ol' dine and ditch too.

Just as the foursome hopped to their feet and bolted for the door, Zane raised his voice. "Stop!" he yelled, then vaulted over the closest table, scattering empty chairs. The teens tore off with Zane in enthusiastic, noisy pursuit.

Later, he'd remember the petit point bookmark that he'd stuffed in his front pocket. Later, he'd recall that wide-eyed, likely panicked expression crossing Harper's face the instant he took chase.

Later, he'd regret the tame little date that he knew now would never be.

"Mom, I'm at work," Harper said, glancing through the half-glass door of her office to the stacks of books and reading nooks set around the library floor as well as the more private study rooms at the rear with their small desks and computers. She'd unlocked the entrance only moments before, but there'd be a steady stream of patrons before long. The board of directors had assured her during her interview that the county's citizens made good and frequent use of the facilities and that hadn't been proved wrong in the couple of months she'd been in Eagle's Ridge.

"That's what I want to talk about," her mother said.

Harper could picture her mother in her lovely sitting room, at the curved-leg, gilded desk with its view of the roses in the side garden. In a tailored suit dress of mint green, or perhaps an understated blue, Patricia Grace likely had a lunch date arranged for later in the day or maybe a meeting set for one of her committees.

"I just don't see you making it out there in the wilds on your own."

Harper smiled. "Urbanite," she said fondly. "There's running water here now, Mother. I've heard tell that electricity will arrive before next winter."

Patricia ignored the gentle sarcasm. "You're not your sister, you know."

Holding onto her patience, Harper straightened the edges of the stack of outgoing mail. "How is Belinda?" she said. "Have you heard from her lately?"

"She's still following that band. Still dating the drummer—or is it the guitarist? I think they're going to Moscow next. And she sold that story she wrote about her life on the road to some magazine."

Harper smiled. Belinda dreamed large and lived large and kudos to their parents who'd managed to survive raising two such different children. "We need to make sure we get copies when it comes out."

"In about six months she said." Patricia cleared her throat, and even that sounded ladylike. "I hope you'll be back home by then."

"Mother…" Harper could feel her about to begin a familiar refrain.

"You didn't have to run away."

I had to get away. "It was past time for a change."

"We could have gone to the Bahamas. Or a girls' trip to Paris." Her voice lowered. "I detest that he chased you away from home."

"Maybe Geoffrey liberated me, Mother."

"I can't see how."

Oh, Harper could see. She'd been one wedding vow away from remaining the quiet, unassuming mouse she'd been her entire life. When Geoffrey Giffin had cut ties with her, it gave her the opportunity to break free of the shell she'd been so comfortably settled in for twenty-seven years.

She didn't think she had it in her to follow rock bands and she'd always love immersing herself in books and finding ways to bring them into other people's lives, but now it was time to try new things.

It had hurt more than a little, hearing that her fiancé considered her too quiet and boring—and to recognize he wasn't altogether wrong. Furthermore, she'd lost some metaphorical skin as she wiggled free of that tidy, contained life in San Francisco, but now she could try a new place and new things.

As her mother sighed—still sounding like the consummate gentlewoman—Harper's gaze wandered back to the interior of the library.

A man strode from the entrance toward the stacks.

Her heart thumped hard against her breastbone. What was Zane Tucker doing here? Last she'd seen him, a couple of days before, he'd been racing out of the diner in a heroic effort to stop a set of teenagers who were trying to get out of paying their bill.

That had followed the astonishing moment when she, Harper "Mouse" Grace, had said to him, *Are you asking me out?*

Who would have thought she had the temerity to voice that thought...or even consider the possibility?

Because Zane, with his confident swagger and his big muscles was everything a woman newly emerging from her comfort zone couldn't handle.

And a woman newly emerging from her comfort zone wouldn't be someone *he* wanted to handle.

She stared at his big hands now, the broad palms and long fingers leading to brawny, bronzed forearms. He had on jeans and a T-shirt that advertised A To Z Watersports. She'd learned it was a local business owned by him and his twin. They rented kayaks and rafts and paddleboards and also guided tours through the downstream rapids as well as hikes in the local mountains.

So those rugged shoulders and flexing muscles were earned the hardworking way, as opposed to only lifting shining weights in some mirror-walled gym. She supposed he might do that too, but his big body shouted outdoorsman.

Now he ambled toward the popular fiction section and she checked out his backside.

The muscles there must get an effective workout too.

"What are you doing, Harper?"

Her mother's voice startled her out of her trance. She edged the back of her hand over her chin to blot any drool accumulated there and shifted her gaze to the surface of her desk. "I'm not doing my job, Mother. So I better get back to it."

The older woman promised to call in the near future and Harper resigned herself to another replay of their conversation. She loved her parents, and it wasn't their fault that her nature had been shy and retiring from the day she was born, but it made it hard for them to let her go…and to believe that she might change.

But I am, she thought, getting up from her desk. Starting with not hiding in her office, even though the man currently prowling the shelves made her pulse beat faster and her stomach jitter.

Wiping her palms along the outside of her dark slacks, she took measured steps in his direction. A few feet away, she halted, staring at the jut of his shoulder blades through the soft cotton of his shirt. Just a glimpse of that was virile enough to make her mouth go dry.

But there was the rest of him too. All the long bones and tousled hair and…and…maleness that the recently renovated library building, despite is vaulted ceilings and airy expanses, could barely contain.

Then he pivoted. And pinned her with the otherworldly blue of his eyes.

Instantly, her nipples tightened as if blasted by cold. But she was hot, suddenly feverish, and despite that she had to pull closer the edges of her black cardigan so he wouldn't see her reaction to him through her bra and lightweight dark gray sweater.

That question from the other day popped into her head. *Are you asking me out?*

It only served to further fluster her, so she pinned on her best librarian smile—kind but impersonal—the one that said she wouldn't judge if someone was seeking information on the treatment of venereal diseases or wanted to be shown the way to the library's collection of same-sex romance novels.

Librarians were like doctors and lawyers that way. Confidentiality was king.

"Can I help you find something?" she asked.

He angled his head, as if she was speaking

another language.

"I've not seen you in the library before," she explained. "Could I point your way to the periodicals? The computers are in the study rooms against the far wall."

"I guess I don't look like the kind of man who reads books."

Zane's tone was as mild as his expression, but Harper heard the words and felt a spear of guilt. God. Talk about judging.

Her face flushed, she could sense the red color crawling over her cheeks. "I'm sorry. I didn't mean to offend you."

One massive shoulder shrugged. "No offense taken."

"Really," she said. "I mean it. I should know better, since I'm a librarian. People make assumptions about me all the time."

"Like what?"

"You know, that I likely have fifteen cats. That I speak only in whispers."

A little smile played around the corners of his mouth. Lord, but he was handsome.

"They don't see the kick-butt mud run girl that you really are?"

She hid her wince. "Exactly." How was she ever going to walk back that claim of hers? It wasn't going to be today, though, when he was looking at her in that way that he had, his gaze so intense it seemed to move the very air between them.

Trying to ignore it, she glanced around his big body, noting the shelf he'd been perusing as she walked up. "Have you read any Westerns?"

"When I was a kid I couldn't get enough of them.

Zane Grey. My grandpa Max brought them to me."

This time a real smile broke over her face. "Of course! Zane Grey. You're not related, are you?"

"Nothing like that. Our mom just got some hair up her ass about using the first and last letters of the alphabet for me and my twin." He shook his head.

"But when you went looking for reading material, there he was."

"There were a lot of titles written by him and I had a lot of time on my hands."

"He was very prolific," Harper said, recalling what she knew of the author's life and career. "Though chasing his dreams and his passions caused him to often ignore his family."

Zane stilled, his jaw tightening. "Yeah," he said shortly. "That happens."

Detecting a mine field, Harper tried tiptoeing immediately out of it. "Which one of his books was your favorite?"

That tense jaw eased. "*Riders of the Purple Sage*. There was a lot I didn't understand about the politics of the story, but there were horses, cattle rustling, and gun battles. Everything a boy could dream of."

"Not to mention revenge and romance," Harper added.

"I was twelve. I don't think I paid too much attention to the romance part," he said, and grinned.

That did it. Her knees softened and her nipples tightened again and she felt...draped in his handsomeness, the weight of his amused gaze and that warm smile cozy and delicious.

Then that grin dropped and his eyes narrowed. "Harper..."

Was he sensing the way he made her swoon? Was

he worried that he was sending the wrong signals or she was mixing them up?

Are you asking me out?

He hadn't answered in the diner, he hadn't brought up anything remotely about it today.

Embarrassed, she stepped around him to give her attention to the books on the shelves. "Have you read any of the Longmire mysteries?"

"I think I've seen the TV show a time or two. I didn't realize there were books."

"Yes, by Craig Johnson." She slid one free and, turning, handed it to him. "This is the first in the series."

He took the novel from her but didn't glance away from her face. "A personal recommendation from the librarian. I feel honored."

Maybe he was teasing. There was a light note to his voice. But there was that heaviness blanketing her again, his male regard touching her everywhere. A shiver worked its way down her spine and she had to lick her lips to moisten them.

Zane's gaze narrowed again as he followed the movement.

Are you asking me out?

Why was that question still in the air? And wait— why couldn't she turn the tables and ask *him* out?

It was a crazy idea...or it was not. Because of course she could do it, a shy woman who was determined to change herself and to try new things, like eat alone at a restaurant and ask a man she felt attracted to out on a date.

Why not?

"Harper?" a voice called in a library hush.

She glanced around, saw that her assistant was

gesturing to her, miming someone was on the phone.

Covering up her mental grimace with a smile, she murmured "Excuse me," to Zane and headed toward her office. Over her shoulder, she was glad to see him open the book she'd recommended and bend his head over the pages. Maybe he'd still be there in a few minutes and she'd broach the subject then.

No, not *broach* the subject. She wouldn't be that tentative. If the man remained in the library once she was free, she'd march right up to him and ask him to join her for coffee. A drink. A meal.

One of those.

The caller was dispatched in less than seven minutes. But as Harper left her office once more, it was to see that Zane had found himself other female companionship. Or, since he hadn't moved, other female companionship had found him.

Trying not to be obvious, she sidled nearer, busying herself with some pamphlets set on the round table near the entrance. Free tax help, a notice about last March's Founders' Day, advice from the fire department regarding the best practices for lighting a Christmas tree.

Obviously it was time to cull the pamphlets on the table.

Harper didn't do anything but make a vague note of this because her attention was focused on the conversation she happened to be eavesdropping upon. Maybe she would have felt bad about it, but the woman was not talking in a library hush. No, not at all.

In a voice full of sympathy, she said, "It's all over town that you're down in the dumps."

He groaned. "Tawny…"

And she would be a Tawny, Harper thought, with her tight jeans and her tight top and her high-heeled boots. Her hair had shine and style and her breasts probably were as fake as the platinum color of her tresses.

More guilt poked at her. Since when was she so catty?

It's a lot better than being mousy, an inner voice intoned.

But there wasn't time to debate it, because Tawny had more things to say. "Honestly, Zane, people get it. Bailey and Adam with their one-and-onlys. You gotta be feeling like the odd man out."

"I don't—"

"I'd volunteer to get your mind off it with a little tumble, I would, but you know that Rick and I just started dating and it feels really good. Solid, even. I don't want to mess that up."

Harper started to like Tawny more than before.

"That's great about you and Rick," Zane murmured. "Now can we—"

"But I thought of his second cousin Janice. She's not seeing anyone at the moment. I can call her, feel her out, see if she's up for a good-time guy and wouldn't get her hopes pinned on a ring or anything near to that. I know it's not in you."

"Great to be so well understood," Zane said, dry as the Sahara.

"But there's one little thing…"

The big man groaned. "She's high-maintenance, is that it? Needs a guy to bring candy on the first date and send flowers the day after?"

"No," Tawny said.

"She has six kids and they all have to come along

with us?"

"No."

"Good, though it's not that I mind kids, it's just that I scare them and the eight of us wouldn't fit in my truck."

Hmm, Harper thought. It seemed he liked kids and didn't want to date a high-maintenance woman. That suited her because she liked kids too. As for the high-maintenance part, her expectations were low. No man had ever brought her flowers or candy. Geoffrey had given her a ring, of course, but then wanted it back when he broke their engagement.

"Janice even has an interesting job. But I have to tell you, the word on the street is, well, she's a dud in the sack."

"A dud in the sack?" Zane repeated.

Finally, Tawny lowered her voice, though Harper could still hear her clearly enough. "According to Andy Smerkman. He dated her when he was visiting over Christmas. Said she's definitely boring in bed."

"Smerkman," Zane said, like a curse. "I don't want to hear any more of this."

Neither did Harper. On swift feet, she moved away, back in the direction of her office. There would be no coffee or drinks with Zane Tucker for her. No dinner or anything else.

No date, one or many.

Because Geoffrey had said she was too reserved. Boring.

Out in the world…as well as in a bed.

And Harper suddenly realized she couldn't bear for Zane Tucker, with that magnificent muscled body and those beautiful big hands, to ever come to the same conclusion about her.

Chapter 3

Zane slid onto a stool at the counter at No Man's Land, wishing the lousy mood the day had left him with would slide away as easily. Mandy planted a root beer in front of him without asking and he sipped at it, thinking he should trek a little farther for a real beer at Baldie's. But he'd promised Adam he'd meet him here.

Closing his eyes, Zane tried to forget all that had gone wrong that morning and afternoon. But damn, he was tired and his aching back served as a constant reminder. The newest A To Z employee, Holly Dillard, hadn't memorized all the items on Gambler's Terror List, and had opened a shipping box that morning. The new personal flotation devices they'd ordered had been packed with bubble wrap. Gleeful, Holly had begun playing with the plastic sheets and the subsequent *pop pop pop* had sent Gambler streaking from the office. He'd broken through the screen door and escaped into the woods.

Zane had gotten muddy from his ankles to his knees during his pursuit, and was too late to stop his fretful canine from trying to smother his anxiety by rolling around in something very dead and very stinky.

Lifting his arm, he sniffed at his skin. Though he'd showered and changed, he swore he could still smell critter carcass on him. Of course, that had meant a bath for Gambler too which had gotten Zane's clean set of clothes more wet than damp.

But then that hadn't mattered, because half an hour later, some teenage hotshot had managed to capsize his single-person kayak a quarter-mile from the dock. Despite his life jacket, the kid had panicked and Zane had been obliged to yank on a wetsuit and swim out with a spare paddle, re-right the vessel, haul the kid into it, and coach the boy in.

Lost: the kid's dignity and one of their more expensive pieces of equipment.

"Don't feel like summer's coming on, does it?"

Zane glanced over at the new arrival. Grandpa Max Tucker, ninety-three years old and still able to hitch himself up on a stool. Following the old man's gaze, he looked toward the bank of windows overlooking the river. The mountains loomed in the background, the peaks wrapped in a blanket of gray.

"Cloudy all day," he confirmed. "Not any actual rain, though."

The old man grunted. "Still the goddamned most beautiful place I've ever seen."

Grandpa Max, John Westbrook, David Bennett, and Will Coleman had traveled to Washington State after their military service in World War II. They'd heard the land was cheap and they'd needed a place to settle. On a hike into the Blue Mountains, the four had looked out over the parcel of land they were considering settling. At a decisive moment, they'd spotted a bald eagle soaring through the sky. Taking it as a sign, they'd bought the land and named the place Eagle's Ridge.

"Beautiful...even from your bedroom at Dad's place?" Zane asked. The old man had been forced into bunking in the small apartment above his son's garage. In March, during a powerful storm, Max's own home had been nearly demolished and he'd had to be rescued in a dramatic and frightening fashion by Ryder Westbrook and his cousin Ford. Thank God for them. Zane and Adam had been in Seattle and didn't know about the danger until it had already passed.

"Nobody likes change," Max grumbled now.

"Not even when it's the beginning of the end of a feud that's lasted way too long?" In the years following the establishment of the town, the Tuckers and the Westbrooks—thanks to Max and John—had entered into a long-running and contentious dispute. If it had not exactly divided the town, it had definitely divided the families. They were now in the first stages of reunification thanks to the romance between Zane's sister Bailey and John's grandson Ryder.

Mandy put a cup of coffee by Max's elbow. He thanked the waitress and then scowled at Zane. "Nobody likes change," his grandfather repeated.

Zane sighed. Hell, maybe that was why he'd been walking around like the clouds were hanging directly over him all day. The fabric of Eagle's Ridge and of his family were indeed altering.

Without thinking, his hand went to his front jeans pocket and he touched the edge of the bookmark he'd tucked inside. His foul mood couldn't be because the image of that pretty librarian continued to haunt him. It couldn't be because he was carrying around that damn wisp of material like it was a talisman.

He should have left it with her at the library two days ago.

But she'd disappeared and he'd felt stupid hanging around like a hound dog hoping for scraps, so here he was, still mooning. Still carrying that damn piece of pretty point or whatever she called it.

The sound of the diner door opening caught his attention and without turning to check on the identity of the entering patron, he signaled to Mandy for another root beer. It was Adam. Zane didn't know how he was certain it was his twin who'd just arrived, but he was.

Just as he was certain his brother felt as tired as he.

Adam gave Max and Zane a short greeting as he took a stool.

"Your rafting gig went long," Zane said. His brother had been on guide duty that day—escorting a book group down the water who'd just read *A River Runs Through It*.

Adam swallowed down some root beer. "They should have taken fly fishing lessons instead. I might have gone deaf due to the squeals and shrieks."

"You could have called me—"

"No need." Adam waved a weary hand. "And Holly did a great job helping me button everything up once we finally made it back."

"Speaking of Holly, we should discuss looking for additional summer employees. The bookings already reserved make it clear we'll need them."

Adam closed his eyes. "Can we not discuss business? I'm about to fall asleep in my root beer foam."

"We shouldn't put it off too long," Zane said mildly. "We don't want to have to resort to begging Jane's help with the watercraft."

That goosed a grin out of his brother. His twin had met the woman in his life when Zane sent her to him...and Adam assumed it was for a guide position—something the interior designer was wholly unsuited for.

"And there's something else we should discuss." Zane glanced over at Max, who'd wandered away from the counter to chat with a silver-haired crony in one of the booths. "I think there's something going on with Dad and Brenda."

Adam dropped his head. "I'm too tired to talk about this."

"They're arguing and I think it's gone beyond bickering."

"Maybe it's none of our business?" his twin asked hopefully.

"Brenda joined an online dating service. Dad said *he's* going to join an online dating service."

Adam's gaze met his own. "Dad's never been serious about dating again."

Yes, which was why Sam's claim had surprised the hell out of Zane too. His dad had never even entirely removed from his house signs of his former wife. Her old aprons hung in the closet. A bottle of Chanel No. 5 perfume continued to sit on the vanity in one of the bathrooms. "He seems pretty serious to me now. What do you think we should do about it?"

"Help him fill out the online form?"

This was from Jane, who'd suddenly appeared behind Adam. She put her arms around his neck and kissed his cheek. "You smell good," she said.

He turned on his stool, his tired expression brightening as he put his hands on her hips. "You are sunshine on a cloudy day."

"You stole that from a song."

"Arrest me. Lock me up in your bedroom and throw away the key." They shared smiles.

Zane made a disgusted sound. "You two are making me want to puke."

"Jealous," Adam said, without taking his gaze off his girl.

Another flurry of activity at the door attracted Zane's attention. His sister Bailey breezed in, hand-in-hand with Ryder Westbrook. "What are they doing here?"

"Didn't our sister tell you?" Adam asked.

"I got your text, instructing me to be here."

"It's Bailey who wanted me to set that up—she has something to run by us. So we're all sitting down for a meal together tonight. Dad and Brenda too, if the dinner rush isn't too bad."

Premonition pricked the back of Zane's neck. "Why don't I think she's going to give us good news?" he murmured.

But then his sister was at the counter and he stirred himself to stand and belatedly kiss Jane's cheek, then Bailey's, following that up with a shake of Ryder's hand. The guy remained the golden boy of Eagle's Ridge, though he'd paid his dues in high school detention too, when Zane and Adam had come to know him outside of the Eagle's Ridge feud.

Now Ryder was likely going to be a permanent

part of the family, judging by the goo-goo eyes his sister sent the other man's way.

Zane stifled yet another sigh. Change.

Grandpa Max returned to his stool and they all milled around generally chatting and catching up. Ryder was in the process of improving and expanding the local airfield. Bailey was taking her many years of chef experience and using them to open a fine-dining establishment in town.

Change, he thought again, scowling.

God, what was wrong with him? All of a sudden, he sounded old. Older than Grandpa. Pretty soon Zane was going to be yelling "Get off my lawn!" at the local kids and then turn into a total curmudgeon.

Who was he to turn his nose up at anybody achieving their dreams or finding that one person who could fill their heart? Why did he find that so irritating?

Unless it was as Adam suggested, a little voice said. Zane was jealous.

Could that be true?

Fine, maybe he was. Maybe a little. Not about the dream part. A To Z was all that for him—a dream job, a dream business. But now he was seeing his future outside of work as the grouchy bachelor uncle that everybody felt sorry for and he didn't especially like it. At every family potluck or holiday dinner, he'd be the one showing up with the bags of ice.

Instead of thoughtful presents for his nieces and nephews, he'd be so out of touch that he'd present them with gift cards for stores where they didn't even like to shop.

It would be up to his brother or his sister to remind him to cut his hair and buy new shirts and someday hire his elderly ass an at-home nurse.

Suddenly, the future sounded even drearier and the room he was in now seemed much too small. He vaulted out of his seat and headed for the diner entrance.

"Hey," Bailey caught his arm. "Where are you going? We're going to sit down together in just a few minutes."

"Can you catch me up later?" He was in no mood to be sociable.

"No," she said, and those prickles tickled his nape again. "I want to tell everyone at once."

"If it's about Ryder—"

"It's about me. And Adam. And you. And Dad. I want you here."

Hell. He ran his hand over his hair. "Okay, okay." A little sister was never someone a guy could say no to. "I'll be right back. I just need some air."

She let him go. He strode to the door and pushed it wide, taking one long step out. Then he was forced to a halt as he came face-to-face with a female face he couldn't seem to forget.

His fingertips slid into his pocket, touched the bookmark. "Oh. Well. Hey, Harper."

"Hey."

He cleared his throat. "I checked out that mystery novel you told me about. Didn't see you around, but the other woman took care of it for me."

"I do hope you enjoy it." Her smile was very professional.

Still, just looking at her pleased him for some unknown reason. He took a breath of the damp air and noted how the evening chill turned the tip of her nose pink. "Are you coming in for food?" he asked, indicating the diner. Maybe the upcoming meal with his family wouldn't be so disturbing if he could watch her from across the room eating while reading.

"I was going to get a salad to go."

"Oh." He rubbed his jaw, wondering how to convince her to take a seat in No Man's Land instead. As a matter of fact, a seat right next to his, so she could distract him during the next hour of Tucker togetherness. Maybe then Bailey's goo-goo eyes and Adam's *You are sunshine on a cloudy day* wouldn't seem so damn annoying.

A couple of women bustled up behind Harper, contemporaries of Brenda's. "Hey, ladies," he said, making room for them to pass. It brought him closer to the librarian and he smelled the sweetness of her hair.

One of them paused before passing through the entrance. "Zane, I've been thinking about you," she said.

He turned. "What? Why?"

"Everybody's aware you need cheering up."

Oh, no. Oh, *hell*, no. "I'm perfectly fine—"

"Maureen. Maureen Goodyear. She's on her third divorce and probably looking for a rebound man. That should do for you since you're not interested in settling down. I'll give her a call for you and—"

"No." Zane's crap mood was back and he reached out for the person who had made him feel good a moment ago. Taking Harper's hand in his, he tugged her close to his side. "I've found my own woman."

The librarian stared up at him, her long-lashed, gray eyes round. And showing sudden concern.

Yeah. Those words coming out of his mouth—and especially how easily they tumbled from it—kind of worried him too.

Harper stood, dumbfounded. Had Zane just said *I've found my own woman*?

At this big fib, the woman he'd been speaking with sent her one quick assessing glance, then disappeared into the diner.

"Okay, that happened," the big man muttered, forking his free hand through his hair. The other still held hers in a firm grip and Harper tried to ignore the warmth traveling up her arm. The tingle running down her spine.

His gaze touched hers, then skittered off. "Uh...sorry?"

"Did you..." Harper swallowed. "Did you just intimate that we..." It seemed impossible to say it plainly.

"I intimated that I don't need any matchmaking help."

"By grabbing me and suggesting that *I'm* your current woman."

"It just popped out," Zane said. "Spur of the moment. Slip of the tongue. You don't know how it's been, everyone in town doling out the poor, poor, pitiful me treatment just because my sister and now my brother are coupled up."

"I see."

He looked her way, his expression turning part-hopeful, part-sheepish. "It'll only get worse if I go in there and you aren't by my side."

"So I should fake being your 'woman' just so you can save face?"

"Ouch." He winced. "It sounds pretty lousy when you put it that way. Really, the fact is, when I stepped out the door a few minutes ago and saw you, I thought how nice it might be to share a meal. Then the other thing happened."

"The lady trying to fix you up."

"She means well. They all mean well, I get that, but it doesn't make it any easier."

"Well, it doesn't seem like you would normally have a hard time getting your own dates."

"Right." Zane squeezed her fingers. "But my temporary dry spell has happened to coincide with the other Tuckers of my generation getting glued to a love interest—and it's looking to be permanent for them."

"Dry spell."

He nodded. "Temporary dry spell."

"Maybe you'd have better luck with the ladies if you didn't make it so patently clear to everyone that you're not interested in settling down." She didn't know why she said that or why she continued to talk in a tone with a distinct edge to it. "Or that you're just a good-time guy who doesn't want a woman he's with to get her hopes pinned on a ring."

He winced again. "You heard Tawny. When she was talking to me in the library."

"Yes." Looking down, Harper tried pulling her fingers free of his hold, but he tightened on them instead. She shifted her gaze to his and felt that pull of his searing blue eyes.

"Don't you think it's better to be honest?" he asked. "Should I lead someone on who's looking for a husband when marriage is not on my agenda?"

Harper had to admit it might be better than being engaged to a woman for two years before finally confessing she's boring and asking for the ring back. "I suppose," she admitted. "Honesty is always the best policy."

He smiled.

She felt it deep in her belly.

"So on that note, Harper Grace, how about we go with this simple truth? I'd like you to come inside and share a meal with me and my family."

The cold of the evening was beginning to penetrate her light coat. She thought of a chilly walk home to her silent condo carrying greens in a recyclable clamshell versus the warmth inside the diner, the golden light that was spilling through the windows, the companionship of the people of her new community. The companionship of this big man with the most compelling eyes she'd ever seen.

Anyone would feel a little yearning, she told herself. It was natural. "Okay."

He gave her a grin, that one she found blinding.

"But you realize no one will believe anything between us is real, right?" she continued. "They won't fall for the fake."

He frowned. "What?"

"Me, you." She waved a hand between them. "Apples and oranges. Uh, triangles and squares. Leopards and...and dust bunnies. We don't go together. They'll see right through the sham."

His mouth opened and before he could say anything, the diner door swung out and his twin leaned through the opening. "You coming, Zane? We're pushing tables together and plates are being served."

"We're coming," Zane replied, his gaze glued to Harper's face. "Harper's going to join me. Going to join us."

"Sure," Adam replied. "But hustle it up."

"Hear it, honey? Big brother says hustle it up."

Within minutes, Harper found herself seated in a chair next to Zane's, the other beside her empty, his family ranged around. Introductions were quick and casual. Mr. Max Tucker, Zane's grandfather, Bailey Tucker, his sister, and the guy she was "getting glued" to, Ryder Westbrook. The Tucker siblings' father, Sam, took a seat far from her at the head of the table and a family friend and the manager of the diner, Brenda Morgan, sat at his right. Harper already knew Adam and Jane.

The waitress passed out platters of the dinner special—steamy mounds of spaghetti and meatballs accompanied by green salads and a basket of garlic bread.

They dug in.

Harper picked up her own fork too and they all devoted their attention to the food for several minutes. Then a conversation started up at the other end of the table, one that Zane ignored. Harper couldn't help but be aware of the silence between the two of them.

And its growing awkwardness.

"This is a very good meal," she finally ventured, casting him a quick glance.

He seemed to have something on his mind, his brows were drawn together. "Dad's recipes are legendary."

"I see—"

"Why would you say that no one would believe anything between us was real?" he demanded, his tone low.

"Um…"

"Leopards and dust bunnies? What the hell is that all about?"

"Well...I..." She made a helpless gesture.

"See?" he said, poking his fork in her direction. "You don't have an answer because it's bullshit, what you said. And I don't like that, a woman running herself down...why? In order to fish for compliments? Do you need that kind of ego-stroking?"

She could only stare at him.

"I sure hope the hell not, because I've already had one beautiful, selfish, game-playing chick in my life and I've sworn to stay clear of any of the rest."

She could only continue staring at him.

"The fact is, your face does something to me and your hair is soft and shiny and I bet you have a great body underneath all those flowy clothes you wear. I like how you look and I'm sure I'm not the only man whose eye has been caught in Eagle's Ridge. So no more dust bunnies talk."

He nodded as if the topic was closed and turned back to his food. "Now eat your dinner."

Still frozen, she sat with her fork poised over her plate, her mind an absolute blank. What could she possibly say? Down the table, a man laughed and she glanced over, only to notice that Zane's twin grinned the exact grin of his brother. Like his eyes were a match for Zane's too.

A question popped into the vacuum that his astounding comments had left behind in her head. "What was it like growing up as a twin?" she asked, grateful that she'd found a way to change the subject. "Did you ever try to change places? Fool people?"

"It's sort of hard to answer that first question since I don't know what it's like to not grow up as a twin," Zane said. "He was just...that other part of me. After high school, we served our country in different branches but I always felt his presence even as I missed him like hell."

Boy, she thought on an inner sigh. Didn't that sound wonderful, having someone who was another part of you? When she'd become engaged to Geoffrey, that's what she'd hoped they'd find in marriage.

"But as for changing places?" Zane was saying now. "No. We could never fool people."

Their hair was different shades, she could see that. "Not even as children, though?"

"Definitely not as children. Adam was a ball of energy—always on the go, but I was a sickly little kid, not well enough to get out much. Asthma. I outgrew it right before high school."

Her gaze darted back and forth between the two brothers. Asthma. It explained all the reading. "I guess you made up for lost time then," she said. "Your muscles are amazing."

And hearing herself, felt heat blossom over her face. She'd put her hands over it if that wouldn't attract even more attention.

Instead of being embarrassed, Zane only gave her another of his smiles. His thigh pressed against hers and he leaned close to her ear. "Is that what you meant by leopard, honey?"

Goose bumps chased down her hot neck. "I...I..."

"What are you whispering to our new librarian?" Adam suddenly demanded, his voice carrying down the table. "You're making her blush."

"Telling her about that time in junior year when lusty Linda King caught us skinny-dipping in the river and then promptly turned around and asked me to the

Sadie Hawkins dance instead of you."

A roll came zinging.

Zane caught it on the fly.

Bailey hooted. "Don't worry, Harper. Lusty Linda King didn't last long. Zane's always had a soft spot for the smart girls like you."

"That's because he sweet-talked them into doing his homework," Adam said.

Taking in the smiling faces of Zane's sister and brother aimed her way, Harper could only come to one amazing conclusion. Seeing her with their brother at the table, they assumed it was a dating type thing between them. And they didn't find it unbelievable that Zane would be interested in her.

She sat a little taller in her chair. "Then I better admit that while I'm a certified spelling whiz, I'm absolutely terrible at calculus."

The others laughed.

"But wait," Bailey said, sobering. "If she's going to be seeing Zane, did anybody think to caution her about the dog? Because he's trouble wrapped in yellow fur."

"He already knocked Harper over on their first meeting," Jane said. "It wasn't pretty."

Bailey frowned. "You've got to get Gambler under control, Zane, he's not a plus on your score sheet. You can be a bull in a china shop and to add to that owning a pet just like you..."

"Geez, Sis, try to keep the compliments down," Zane grumbled.

"One more warning, Harper," Adam said. "Don't make any bets with my brother. They only lead to destruction—"

"Or detention," Ryder finished for him.

"And one is going to land him in big trouble someday," Bailey said, narrowing her eyes at Zane. "Remember I said that."

"Or maybe not." Harper stole a glance at Zane's annoyed expression, then directed her attention to the others at the table. "Consider Dr. Seuss."

A moment of silence passed.

Then Zane's mouth twitched, his expression lightening. "Okay, honey, we've considered Dr. Seuss. What next?"

"*Green Eggs and Ham*. The book," she clarified.

"I didn't think you were suggesting a new dish for Dad's diner." Zane sat back in his chair. "What about *Green Eggs and Ham*?"

"It was written on a bet. With his publisher," she said. "*The Cat in the Hat* uses 236 words. The wager was that he couldn't write a book with fifty or less."

"Fifty or less," Ryder repeated.

Harper knew her smile was triumphant. "And to date, that book has sold over eight million copies."

Sam Tucker laughed, shaking his head. "I'm going to have to find ours. It's got to be around the house somewhere."

Zane half-turned in his chair, and he studied her face, his gaze warm. Her breath caught. "Aren't you something?" he marveled.

"I-I don't know what you mean." His intense regard was causing a flutter in her belly.

"You stuck up for me," he murmured. "That's pretty sweet. I was okay with their pestering, it's what Tuckers do, but nobody's ever felt the need to come to my defense since I turned fifteen and gained fifty pounds and five inches in half a year."

At that, he reached out a big hand and brushed

her hair behind her ear. Aware that they were the center of attention for the table, she struggled to hide the shiver he caused. But battling it only served to make her feel it more keenly, more widely, so that the secret caress of his fingertip along the curve of her ear felt as if he was tracing other intimate folds and other sensitive stretches of flesh.

"Zane," she whispered, hoping it sounded like a protest instead of an entreaty.

From several seats away, she saw that Brenda was beaming at her. "I like Harper," she declared. "I like Harper for Zane."

Uh-oh. This shared meal wasn't supposed to signal a true Harper-and-Zane anything. Except her pulse was stuttering and heat was gathering beneath her clothes and nothing could stop Harper's imagination—not her good sense nor life experience—from wondering just exactly what real with Zane Tucker might be like.

Chapter 4

Conversation at the table buzzed, but Zane didn't hear it as he gazed into Harper's upturned face. God, what made her so damn appealing to him? Again, he stroked the curve of her small ear with the edge of his thumb and watched a tiny quiver roll through her small figure. Even beneath the long sweater she wore with a blouse and slacks, he could sense the effect of his touch on her.

Yeah. So damn appealing.

He'd never seen such fine-pored skin, a creamy color that couldn't hide a rising blush. Her eyes, gray as so many spring mountain skies, stood out in contrast to that sweet pink on her cheeks.

Then a voice penetrated his concentration.

"I'm with you, Brenda," Bailey said. "I like Harper and Zane."

His hand dropped, breaking the connection between him and the librarian. He briefly closed his eyes and cursed himself for forgetting what he already knew. There would be no Harper and Zane. The humming attraction between them needed to be ignored or severed or smothered—something—because she was a woman who needed a man capable of providing a forever.

Everybody knew the bull in the china shop could only be counted on to break things.

"Will you excuse me, please?" Harper said now, scooting out her chair without meeting his eyes. "I won't be long."

She didn't wait for his response and he watched her quickly glide between the tables in the direction of the restrooms.

Then he turned his attention back to his family, who had moved on to a discussion of Ryder's progress on the airfield. As Zane tuned into the conversation, Adam glanced over, saw that he was paying attention and cleared his throat.

The table went quiet.

"Bailey," his brother said. "You brought us together tonight for a reason. Plan to share anytime soon?"

His sister glanced at Ryder who gave her a little nod. Her gaze went to where her plate had been before Mandy cleared it and all the others away. "You know I'm opening the restaurant at the end of the month."

Grandpa Max snorted. "Yes, and half the town is chuffed that a real New York chef is going to treat us to some fine dining, as if the diner isn't good enough for their fancy palates."

"Grandpa," Bailey protested.

"It's the influence of the snooty Westbrooks," he muttered, then shot a look across the table at the much younger man seated there. "Uh, sorry, Ryder."

He looked more amused than offended. "Wait until you have a taste of her beef bourguignon, Max, and you might find your own palate just got a little bit fancier."

Zane stepped in before his grandfather could put in another word. "Back to what you were going to say, Sis?" he prompted.

This time, Bailey's gaze turned to their father. "I'm going to make an event of it—opening night."

"Sounds like a fine idea," Sam said in an approving tone. "I'll close the diner early to cut down on your competition."

She smiled at that. "I'm hoping you'll come, too. There'll be a soft opening for friends and family only on Thursday night as well."

"Of course." Sam beamed at her. "I wouldn't miss it—or the official open either."

"Somebody else doesn't want to miss those special nights either," Bailey said.

Oh, crap. Zane suddenly knew why he'd had spiders walking over him all night. Deep down he'd known bad news was coming, and from the hesitant look on his sister's face, he could guess exactly what kind of bad news.

"Don't everyone freak out," his sister continued, her shoulders tense. "I know this isn't what you all might want, but Mom's saying she's wants to be there when I welcome everyone to Blue Moon…and I'd like that too."

The sudden quiet that followed was deafening.

At the end of March, Bailey had told him and Adam about their mother's interest in returning for her Eagle's Ridge restaurant debut, but neither one of them had put much stock in it. But now their mom had actually committed for real? He traded a glance with Adam, who raised his brows and shrugged.

Then Sam spoke up, his expression giving nothing away. "You're saying that Vicky is returning here?"

She'd left seventeen years before, following her dreams to Hollywood. For eight years she'd starred as the mother on *Mother May I,* a popular TV drama centered around a family, even as those choices she made ruined her very own in Eagle's Ridge.

But apparently Bailey had it in her to forgive. As to what Sam thought...

"She called to chat a while back, Dad." Bailey licked her lips. "We're reconnecting. I...I'm glad."

Ryder rose from his chair and came around the table to stand behind Zane's sister. He put his hands on her shoulders, a certain sign of support. She tilted her chin to glance up at him and smiled a little. "I want her to get to know Ryder."

After another silent moment, Sam nodded. "I get it, honey. I'm glad she'll be here to celebrate with you if that's your wish."

Then he abruptly stood and strode in the direction of the kitchen.

Zane jumped up, knocking over his water glass in his haste to follow his father.

He found Sam in the small breakroom, staring at the wall as if the meaning of life was written upon it.

"Dad?" Zane said, in a voice as hushed as he could make it.

"Hmm?" He sounded a million miles away.

"Are you okay?"

Turning, Sam grimaced. "That should be my line. What about you, Son?"

"I'm good."

His dad slid his hands into the front pockets of his jeans. "You haven't seen your mother in a long time, have you?"

"No."

"Do you communicate with her at all?"

"Not since that time I went to LA right after the divorce. Instead of all the 'fun' she promised, she shoved a handful of take-out flyers at me and a fistful of cash."

Sam nodded, as if he understood the situation. "Something came up on the set?"

"They had to re-shoot a scene or a bunch of scenes, what do I know? Only that I didn't see her until she drove me back to the airport at the end of the weekend."

"You never said." His father's head bent as if he thought his shoes now held the key to the world's secrets. "But I'm sure she loves you, Zane."

"When I was that bed-bound asthmatic little kid, she was great. Entertained the hell out of me so I didn't mind so much that I couldn't keep up with Adam. But the minute I managed to kayak across the river without getting out of breath, it seemed she was on the first outbound plane to that producer who'd seen her in the community theater play."

"None of us could keep her here."

"Not even you, Sam," Brenda said, walking into the room.

He looked up. "I figured that out a long time ago, Bren."

"But you held onto the hurt. It's not been healthy."

His expression turned annoyed. "Like you

haven't nursed your heartache over losing Vince."

Zane wanted to wince at the mention of Brenda's husband, killed in action a long time ago. But Brenda herself didn't blink. "And I realized that on my own when the calendar told me it's been ten years since he passed. Now I'm working on moving on."

Sam's face softened and he crossed to her, taking one of her hands in both of his. "Brenda, I'm sorry," he said, his voice gruff. "I shouldn't have lashed out at you."

"I understand." She slipped out of his hold and took her turn at staring at her shoes. "You're in pain."

"I don't know what the hell I feel," Sam muttered, shaking his head. "Unsettled. Unbalanced, but I don't think that I can pin that on Vicky. It's been a while now since things haven't been the same. Felt quite the same."

Brenda's head jerked up. "Oh?"

They looked into each other's eyes a long, silent moment. Long enough for Zane to get decidedly third-wheel vibes. Crap.

He didn't think he could take more alterations to the Tucker family circle.

"How was your date the other night?" Sam asked Brenda now, his voice almost pillow-talk low. "Did you enjoy yourself? Did that chump you went out with act like a gentleman?"

"Chump?" Her face flushed, Brenda smiled a little. "You don't even know the man, Sam."

"I don't want to know him," Sam said, commandeering the woman's hand again. He tugged her closer. "But do I want to know something else…"

Oh, boy. They clearly had forgotten he was in the room. Zane backed out quickly, wondering if it was better that he heard nothing from the pair he left behind. Which was an improvement—more bickering or a telling silence?

But that question evaporated from his mind when he pushed through the kitchen door and spied Harper on her way toward the diner's exit. "Hey, where are you going?" he called out, hurrying to her.

She halted. "Sorry, Adam said you were with your dad. I should have waited to say goodbye and thank you, but I didn't know how long you'd be and...and I should get going."

"Not without a couple of escorts. You walked, right?"

"I like walking."

"Gambler and I do too. Give me have a second to get him. We'll meet you right outside."

"It's not necessary—"

"Yes, it is," he said firmly. "It's dark. We'll accompany you."

After collecting Gambler from the storeroom, he went out the rear to find Harper waiting at the front, her coat fastened up to her throat and her hands deep in the pockets. His dog lunged for her, but he pulled back, bringing Gambler closer to his knees. "Clearly our need to sign up for deportment classes has not abated."

He thought he heard Harper's stifled laugh as they set off in the direction of her condo.

"I liked your family," she ventured minutes later. "I recognized your grandfather. He comes into the library from time-to-time to read *La Fenêtre*."

At his inquiring look, she continued. "It means 'The Window' and is a weekly English language newspaper focused on French news."

"Ah. Grandpa Max has a special interest there. He was in Paris right after it was liberated during World War II."

"Then I certainly won't let our subscription lapse." She dug her chin deeper into her coat.

"Cold?" he asked.

"I'm okay."

But he put his free arm around her anyway, tucking her close to his body and matching his steps to hers. Gambler seemed happy enough to amble on his other side, which made for a cozy walk through Zane's favorite town in the world.

With a woman who fit against him in a way he shouldn't like so much.

He cleared his throat. "Sorry I deserted you back there." Should he say more? Explain?

"Bailey told me she delivered some news that may have upset your father. Or upset you."

"She did?" His sister had a big mouth.

"I think she felt she had to say something when you weren't at the table."

"Oh. Right."

Then he felt the gentle jab of an elbow. "*Are* you upset?"

Only because I can't start getting used to the feel of you in my arms. "Nah. I was worried about my dad, mostly." He took in a breath. "Our mom left town a long time ago for a career in Hollywood. Left the family, divorced our dad. She's coming back for Bailey's restaurant opening and I haven't seen her in years and years."

"You're okay with it?"

Zane hesitated. He wasn't one much for talking about his feelings and he couldn't remember the last time a woman had probed for them.

Bulls in china shops weren't known for actually having them, he supposed.

"Zane?" Her hand withdrew from one of her pockets and she reached up to pat his wrist draped casually over her shoulder. "Are you okay?"

"When I was a kid, I told you I was sickly."

"I remember." Her hand moved down to squeeze his.

"She was great at keeping me occupied, I'll say that for her." He hesitated again. "But then I started getting well and her interest in home seemed to wane in proportion. One of the last things she said to me was 'You don't need me anymore.' For a while I thought it was my fault she left us. That I'd driven her away purely because I started being able to breathe normally."

Harper's feet halted, making his do the same. Then she turned into his body, so that his arm dropped from her shoulder. Yet they remained close together, the buttons of her jacket nearly touching him.

In the moonlight he could see her big eyes trained on his face. "Tell me you don't believe that anymore."

"I don't." For some reason he cupped her cool cheek in his warm hand. "I…"

Whatever he would have said next was lost when Gambler, impatient or just impulsive, leaped up, his front paws to Zane's shoulder blades. He stumbled forward, gripping Harper to keep his balance. She gripped him to keep hers.

And just like that, their mouths found each other's. At the first taste of her, Zane lost his head.

It was the fragrance of her hair, he thought. The delicate touch of her tongue when it met his. Or the perfect way she melted against him when he scooped her closer to his body, his free hand on her sweet, rounded ass.

He angled his head, taking the kiss deeper and she moved in, her arms going around his neck. She was little, so he had to take her to her toes to get the deepest of kisses, but she didn't hesitate, making a soft, sexy noise in the back of her throat.

Breaking the kiss so they could take a breath, he nuzzled along the soft skin of her cheek and found her ear. He tongued there, feeling the shiver he set off streak down her body. Her hands shoved into his hair and she brought his lips back to hers.

The small sign of aggression made him grin inside even as he dove into another hot, wet, drugging kiss.

Then two loud honks penetrated the smoky haze in his head. His eyes opened and he shifted his gaze to the street. A slow-moving truck was rolling by.

"Hey, Zane!" a voice yelled through an unrolled window. "Find a bed."

"Dude." Another voice. "Or at least the privacy of a study room in the library."

"Oh, hell," he muttered, jerking back to end the kiss.

"What?" asked Harper, sounding dazed even as he put her away from him. "What is it?"

"Morons," he said, gazing at the tail lights receding in the distance. He'd known not to let this attraction get as far as kissing. *Hell.*

"I'm sorry, Harper." He glanced over, trying not to notice how pretty her mouth was, swollen now. From him. "Really sorry."

"It's just silly teasing," she said then, and it was

obvious she was trying to regather her dignity as she stepped away and smoothed her hair. She didn't look at him as she fiddled with her collar, embarrassment in every gesture. "Kids making fun."

He looked on her with pity. "Harper."

"What?" She glanced up, alerted by his tone. "What is it?"

"After what I said to that friend of Brenda's in the diner tonight…about finding my own woman?"

A hesitation. "Yes?"

"Followed up by getting caught necking in the dark?"

A second, longer hesitation. "Yes?"

"In a small, close-knit town like this one—we might as well take out an ad. Everybody will have heard by tomorrow." He paused, waiting for the onset of guilt. This wasn't right for her. *He* wasn't right for her, despite the fire in those kisses and how bad he wanted to hold her close again and grind his hard cock against her flat belly—which pointed out exactly how he was wrong for her because he was the untamed and undomesticated kind of man who wanted to grind his cock against the shy little librarian.

"Zane." He heard that shy little librarian swallow. "Everybody will have heard what exactly?"

"That you've got a man now, Harper." He hauled in a breath. "And for better or worse, that man is me."

Harper strolled through the stacks of books in the direction of the periodicals, taking the long way around in order to avoid the shelves of Westerns. Running her gaze over Zane Grey novels wouldn't help matters, she knew. It had been bad enough yesterday when she'd been putting together a display of alphabet books in the children's section. So many darn Zs, each one of them calling up visions of the person she was determined to put from her mind.

You've got a man now, Harper.

Of course she did not.

No matter what he said, dust bunnies and leopards did not belong together and nobody would be fooled to think differently by witnessing some meaningless lip-lock in the moonlight.

Don't think about that. Don't think about him.

She bent to straighten a stack of newsmagazines on a slanted shelf, the hem of her long cardigan swinging out. *I bet you have a great body underneath all those flowy clothes you wear.*

Closing her eyes, she tried pushing that memory away too.

She didn't have much luck until there came the distinctive click and *whoosh* of the library's entrance door swinging open. Ah, her first patron of the day!

Eager for the distraction, Harper hurried to greet the visitor, hoping to be presented with a thorny research problem or put on the hunt for a special book she could retrieve from the inter-library loan system. Though she was naturally reserved around strangers, in her capacity as librarian she had professional obligations and actually found it fairly easy to engage with people within the world of books.

Her smile on, she came around a corner to see the manager of No Man's Land and unofficial member of the Tucker family, Brenda Morgan. She was dressed for the cool, late spring weather in jeans, a plaid shirt with the tails hanging out, and sheepskin-lined boots. Her direct gaze made clear what—who—was the target of her visit.

Harper considered making a break for her office. Had the other woman heard about the kiss?

But Brenda was already mere feet away. "Hello, there."

"Um, hello," Harper responded, hoping it wasn't a blush that was heating her face. "Can I help you with something?"

"I hoped we might have a chat."

Oh, no, Harper thought. The speculative light in the other woman's eyes told the truth of it. She'd definitely heard about the kiss. And though two nights ago Brenda had said *I like Harper for Zane*, likely she'd come to her senses since then and realized they were a total mismatch. They didn't belong in the same league.

But she seemed to be a kind woman. Probably Brenda thought she should warn Harper off—signal to the librarian that upon further thought she realized the librarian didn't have the feminine chops to take on a man as virile as Zane Tucker.

Brenda smiled again. "I won't take up much of your time."

The phrase made Harper inwardly cringe. Those were the exact words Geoffrey had said that evening he'd shown up on her doorstep following her giddy and gabby phone call all about how the wedding venue had been secured. She'd been floating on air and then he'd arrived and pulled the clouds out from under her feet. *I won't take up much of your time* led to *I want to end our engagement*.

The fall to earth had *hurt*.

"Are you all right?" Brenda asked now, concern entering her eyes.

"Of course, yes." Harper drew in a steadying

breath and half-turned. "A chat you said? My office, or—"

"Here is fine," Brenda said, gesturing to a nearby grouping of chairs.

They both sat and Harper automatically tidied the stack of Get Dirty for Books flyers on the table between them. Then she looked up to catch the other woman studying her, wearing an expression Harper couldn't interpret.

So she decided to grab the tiger by the tail. "Look, I think I know the purpose of your visit." *To save me from potential heartache. To warn me against harboring dreams that can't come true. But I don't need to be cautioned. I'm aware he's too much man for me and—*

"It's because I thought you might have questions for me," Brenda said.

Harper's brows shot together. "What?"

"The dinner party ended abruptly the other night and I want to apologize for that—as well as explain in case you were left wondering what was going on."

"Oh." She *was* a kind woman. "You don't have to worry about that. Zane filled me in."

Brenda's pretty green eyes rounded. "Really?"

"Yes. He explained about his mom's return for Bailey's restaurant opening. I think he's mostly okay with it."

The older woman wore her dark hair in a long braid that nearly reached her waist. She drew it over her shoulder now, and toyed with the end absently, a slight frown on her face. "He shared that with you?"

"He said he used to blame himself for her leaving, but he knows now that wasn't true."

Brenda's mouth dropped. "He shared *that* with

you?"

"Yes."

"Well." A genuine smile broke over the diner manager's face. "Well, well, well. I believe my work here is done."

Harper tilted her head, not following. "I don't understand."

"Men aren't always aware of their feelings or even if they are, they aren't very keen about sharing them."

I've been thinking this for a while now, Harper. You're just too…humdrum for me. While she'd been living in her head, concocting tulle-fueled fantasies of a romantic ceremony followed by a lifetime of wedded bliss, Geoffrey had been dating on the side for the previous six months, entertaining himself with a string of apparently exciting and interesting one-night women.

"I've experienced that myself," Harper admitted.

"But I do believe the Tucker men are making progress." Brenda seemed to head off into her own mini-daydream, her attention wandering away. "Even Sam."

Interesting. Like all librarians, Harper could sense a good story. "You're talking about Zane's dad?"

Brenda's gaze remained unfocused. "You're not the only who got kissed the other night," she murmured.

Even more interesting! But before Harper could figure out what to say next, Brenda came back to herself. Her gaze snapped to Harper's even as her face took on a delicate pink. "I should stop yakking your ear off," she said, standing.

It had only been a short conversation, but Harper

stood too. "Sure. Is there anything else?"

The other woman hesitated, then glanced around. "Actually, could you point me in the direction of your books on photography?"

"Certainly, follow me." As they walked, Brenda shared about the class she was taking in the subject at the community college.

"I needed a new hobby," she said. "Frankly, I need a new me...and I'm getting there."

"It's why I came to Eagle's Ridge," Harper said, surprised to find herself confessing. "I was a little too comfortable in my old shell."

Brenda patted her arm. "Zane might be just the man to yank you out of it."

Since Harper didn't know how to respond to that, she did what she did best, kept quiet and helped the older woman find the right book for her needs. Soon enough, Brenda was leaving the library and Harper kept herself busy during the next hours with patrons and paperwork.

By afternoon, she congratulated herself on the few number of times she'd had to push that Tucker man from her mind, but on the tail of that thought she saw someone new walk into the library. Jane McAllen, carrying two carryout cups.

Like Brenda before her, she came straight to Harper. "Do you have time for tea?"

"Um..." The other woman exuded chic with her dark hair and eyes and stylish, form-fitting clothing. She was an interior designer by profession and if there was ever anyone to make Harper feel washed-out and plain, it was beautiful Jane. But she wore a bright smile and she'd always been friendly when they'd met, so Harper could hardly refuse her now.

"Sure." She led the way into her office and they settled into the two visitor chairs.

Jane handed her one of the steaming cups. "Chamomile."

"Thank you." Harper sipped.

"I thought we should get better acquainted," Jane said.

Oh, no. Harper tensed. Was this because of Zane? That was really going nowhere and she needed to communicate that she didn't expect it would either. "Well, I—"

"I'm new to town, you're new to town."

Harper relaxed. A new friend wouldn't be bad.

"And apparently we're dating twins."

"I wouldn't call it—"

"I met him first, you know. Zane."

Sitting up straighter, Harper couldn't resist asking for more. "You did?"

"Uh huh. I was looking for work so he sent me to Adam, who, by the way, jumped to conclusions about me and was very rude about it." But the thought seemed to put a shine in her eyes.

"He doesn't seem like a rude kind of man."

"Sparks," Jane said, with a wave of her hand and smiled. "He didn't want to feel them, especially for me because he could sense I was keeping secrets."

"Ah." That whole debacle when innocent Jane had become a pawn in a revenge plot.

"Their mother did a number on them when she left and they all have their issues," Jane continued. "Zane, included. His are compounded by some girl who did another number on him when he was in his early twenties."

She wasn't going to pry, Harper ordered herself.

She was going to keep quiet like she usually did, quiet as a library mouse. But her mouth had other intentions. "There was some girl who did a number on him?"

Jane shrugged. "Sorry. I don't have any details, it's just something Adam picked up on. Speaking of which, I need to get going. We're meeting for a late lunch."

As she stood, Harper was struck again by the other woman's clear sense of style. Her shiny hair swung about her shoulders and she slid an elegant bag over her arm. "Are you still planning to do that?" Jane asked, one perfectly filed—though not polished—fingernail pointing to a Get Dirty for Books flyer on the desk.

"Oh. I…" It was the moment to admit it had been a man-induced, pride-saving, totally substance-less declaration. And then she remembered when she made it, while under the influence of all Zane's beautiful manliness and those mesmerizing blue eyes.

Even in the dark, with only the moon to light the night, those eyes held power over her. Which explained why she'd kissed him and wanted to keep on kissing him, even when those yahoos on the street had honked their horn.

Standing in her office, she recalled every hot moment of being in his arms and the way he made her feel…needy, excited. Exciting.

Never humdrum.

But she wasn't supposed to be daydreaming about Zane or his kisses or how her knees had been unable to hold her up and how she'd reveled in his size and strength, she reminded herself. It wouldn't do at all to set herself up for another heartbreak.

So she blinked herself out of the reverie and sucked in a deep breath. God, she definitely needed something to take her mind off what couldn't be. Who she couldn't have.

A task. A hobby.

Photography, or…

She looked down at the fundraising flyer and then up at Jane, still waiting for her reply. "Of course, I'm going to compete in the event," she said, latching onto the idea like a lifeline. "As a matter of fact, I'm going on a training run as soon as I get off of work."

That day, Harper's schedule allowed her to leave the library in the late afternoon and with the sun setting later each evening there was no reason she couldn't follow through with that promised run. Except, of course, that she'd never "run" since fourth grade when she'd regularly been chased on the playground by a big bully named Bridget Marino. So it would be more of a jog, she told herself as she laced up the athletic shoes she wore for weekend visits to the local farmer's market.

Wearing leggings, a sports bra, and an oversized tunic that skimmed her thighs and covered her rear, an outfit she'd worn on those spin-class beach cruises, she performed a few stretches outside her condo, starting with reaching her arms to the sky and ending by pulling her heels toward her butt. She gave a searching look at the clouds overhead, decided it didn't look like rain, and also decided she couldn't procrastinate a moment longer.

Reminding herself of her hobby resolution, she started off, heading down the road that led out of Eagle's Ridge proper, parallel to the river. At first it went well, and she didn't push it, going steady and breathing easy of the fresh air that left the hint of a spring green taste on her tongue. It almost managed to eradicate the memory of Zane's flavor in her mouth and the manly smell of him in her lungs, the feel—

No. She pushed that all away and concentrated on the tempo of her feet and the pattern of her breaths. One-two. In-out. As she settled into a rhythm, she let her mind spin off, daydreaming as she so often did. Telling herself a story.

This could be my life.

She could have a new identity, truly be that new Harper that she'd left San Francisco to find. Not humdrum, boring Harper, but a runner. One of those sinewy-armed, toned-calf women with washboard stomachs so flat their running shorts barely hung from their hips.

She'd lose her curvy behind—something Geoffrey had once claimed to admire—but that would be a small price to pay because no one back home would ever think she'd run away when she told them—and showed them with that body—that she'd gone to Eagle's Ridge to become an actual runner. It sounded strong. Cool.

Five more minutes passed and she turned off the main road onto a skinnier one that was bordered by evergreens on either side. Her feet continued slapping on the pavement. Her air continued moving in and out of her lungs.

Okay, she thought as time went on. Maybe *she'd* not be boring in her new identity, but the repetitive nature of this new activity was striking her as a trifle...tedious. In beach cruise spin class, at least there'd been Jimmy Buffett and the Beach Boys coming through the speakers and the surfer dude-ish instructor helping the time pass with stories of his epic rides on the local waves.

On her next run, she decided, she'd plug earbuds into her phone and find a diverting playlist. No…she'd listen to an audio book.

Relief whooshed through her, taking with it the minor tightness in the muscle in her right calf. Running could be made more pleasurable when combined with her favorite activity of reading.

For a while she kept the boredom at bay by mentally sifting through the books in the library's audio catalog. What would work best on a run? That non-fiction historical tome she'd been meaning to open? The self-help book about the best way to clean house?

Ugh. Neither seemed right for a runner girl.

It had to be a thriller, then. Listening to a story about a serial killer would give her the incentive to keep herself in shape and to improve her pace. Pretty soon she'd be an award-winning runner, fast enough to elude all the bad guys. No Eagle's Ridge Butcher would be able to catch her.

For a few more steps she tried picturing the Eagle's Ridge Butcher. Dirty jeans, a black hoodie pulled over his head, nearly to his eyebrows. His murderous specialty was—

"Hey, Harper."

At the sound of a male voice, she shrieked and nearly jumped out of her shoes. The Butcher! Heart in her throat, she gathered her will for an all-out sprint and took one swift look at…

Zane Tucker.

Her hand flew to her chest. "Oh my God."

He was in the driver's seat of a big shiny black truck that he'd steered toward the wrong side of the road so she could see him clearly framed in the open window. Riding shotgun was Gambler, his window open too, his head hanging out.

Her heart continued to hammer. "You're not the Butcher of Eagle's Ridge," she said, breathless.

"Uh, no." His lips twitched, those lips that had been so hot and hard on hers. "I don't know who you mean. There's ol' Saul behind the deli counter at the market. Is that—"

"No, I mean the serial killer."

He blinked those incredible blue eyes.

"The serial killer I made up," she explained, beginning to feel foolish.

"You made up a serial killer."

"As a motivation, you know, to run faster."

A little smile curved his mouth and there was amusement written all over his face. "You live in your head a lot, don't you?"

Geoffrey had said that too, like it was a problem, which it had been because it was why he'd been able to elude detection during six months of consecutive dating those other more exciting and interesting women. She hadn't noticed him drawing away when she was deep in her tulle-fueled daydreams. Yes, she lived in her head a lot.

"I'm a librarian," she said, as if that explained it, and it kind of did.

"A librarian who tells herself stories about serial killers."

She grimaced. "You make me sound odd."

"I find you fascinating." He grinned.

It was that white, bright, blinding grin of his and

it did something to her stomach, causing the whole of it to jitter. Okay, time to get back to the task at hand. "Well," she said, starting off again. "Have a good day."

Instead of taking the hint and moving along, he hardly touched the accelerator at all, the huge truck prowling beside her, keeping to her pace. "We should talk about that kiss," he said, his tone casual.

It was her aim not to be thinking about the kiss, let alone talking about it!

She glanced over, saw that one of his wrists was draped over the top of the steering wheel, the other arm propped on the bottom frame of the window, the pose of every hot teenage boy she used to moon over in high school. Those boys who had never looked back, let alone put their lips to hers.

"It was nothing," she said. "I've already forgotten it." Picking up her speed, she continued on, trying to escape the lie—and him.

Zane merely goosed the gas to keep up with her.

Harper tried to go a faster speed, but it was becoming clearer by the second that while good intentions had energized her during the beginning of the run and adrenaline had kept her invigorated once Zane had shown up, both were fizzling out with each step.

"You should take a rest," he suggested. "Walk for a while."

"No." She might have wanted to add that he could move it along and leave her alone, but she didn't have the breath for it.

"We're going to have to talk about that kiss."

"No. I'm busy."

"Busy killing yourself. You won't be able to

move tomorrow."

"I'll manage."

"My house is on this road…a quarter mile from here," he said.

She grunted, the only response she could make.

"I bet you can't make it there…that you'll have to quit before you reach my front door."

Her eyes narrowed and she glared at him. "Not…quitting." Pride made her take the next step, and then the next, and then another.

"If you make it to my front door, I'll share my Chinese take-out. Get you a cold beer, too."

Cold beer. She didn't often drink beer, but this one she could see. Almost taste. "If. I. Don't?"

"Make it, you mean?"

She nodded.

"Then you'll let me kiss you again."

Of course, Harper dragged herself to Zane's front door.

As he stepped out of his truck, he was shaking his head. "Honey, you look wiped."

Half-bent, she had her palms on her knees, struggling to catch her breath. "I like Chinese." *I need to avoid more kissing from you.*

They didn't get to the contents of the white paper bag he carried right away though. First he insisted on getting her a fleece sweatshirt of his and directing her toward the downstairs bathroom of his A-frame cabin. "You don't want to catch a chill with sweat against your skin. Take off your top, your bra. Tights too, this shirt of mine will keep you decent."

Award-winning runner girls would not blush when a man mentioned the word "bra," she reminded herself, and entered the spacious tiled space. Quickly she stripped off the damp garments, used a washcloth to freshen up, then pulled his fuzzy garment over her head.

It draped her to her knees and smelled like him.

She brought the too-long sleeve to her nose, inhaled deeply, and then quickly let her arm drop, feeling a spurt of shame.

At least she didn't snoop in the medicine cabinet, she thought, and walked back out to the expansive main room, trying to feel "decent" despite wearing only a pair of panties and his oversized garment. From the other end of the space, by the kitchen, Gambler's head shot up. Then he came loping toward her, his sweeping tail knocking remotes off a table, as well as sending sections of a piled newspaper flying into the air. She shrank back against the bathroom door, unable to prevent herself from cowering before the dog's oncoming assault.

Out of nowhere, Zane appeared and grabbed the dog by the collar. "That's no way to put a lady at her ease," he said to the animal.

"I think he wants to eat me."

"Nah, I just fed him dinner while you were in the bathroom." He marched the Lab forward and had him sit near her feet. "He's only eager to say hello again."

Harper stared down at the dog. "Hello," she said.

"He's had a bad day," Zane shared. "Some teenagers in the parking lot at A To Z were on skateboards and bikes, towing each other around with ski ropes. When I wouldn't let him run for the trees, he cowered under my desk all day."

The story made her take a second look. Perhaps the dog didn't look so much ravenous as misunderstood. With a tentative hand, she patted the top of his head, the fur soft as a bunny's. "Poor Gambler."

"I've got your beer ready and waiting," Zane said now.

She looked up, saw the way his gaze had settled on her face, and had the sudden thought that maybe it was *he* who wanted to eat her up. A Red Riding Hood-shiver worked its way down her spine. "Um, perhaps I should go on home."

"I'll drive you—after the beer, after you eat."

Already she felt an oncoming soreness and stiffening in her muscles. On a sigh, she acquiesced. At a small table between the kitchen area and the living room space, they dished out food—chow mein, sweet and sour, egg rolls. Harper found she was famished and hardly noticed that Gambler had camped himself at her side, his chin resting on her bare foot.

"We should talk about the kiss," Zane said again, as they polished off the final bites of their meal.

Stubborn man. Instead of saying so, she lifted her chin and glanced around the room with its wood-paneled walls and wide windows. "You don't have any deer heads." Then she aimed her gaze to the polished wood floors. "Where are the bear rugs?"

He was grinning at her, as if her comments amused him. "I don't hunt much anymore. I lost my taste for shooting things."

Her eyes widened.

"I was in the Army," he explained. "Ten years, until I hurt my shoulder and decided it was time to get out and get back to Eagle's Ridge."

"I've met more than one person in town with a military service record."

"It's a tradition around here. The area was settled by four World War II vets, Grandpa Max included, and a lot of the young men—and some of the young women—follow in those footsteps."

Harper frowned. "You were hurt?" She ran her gaze over his wide shoulders, trying to see through his shirt to any damage that might linger. She hated that he might have some residual pain.

"In the past, honey, so you don't have to wear that sad expression because of me. I'm good."

But he'd lost his taste for shooting things. Maybe not as good as he thought, and then she recalled what Jane said, that some woman had "done a number on him."

But Harper had to forget all that, as it was none of her business, leopard and dust bunny prohibiting it from being so. "I'm not wearing a sad expression," she said, probably lying, but she wasn't anywhere near a mirror.

He smiled once more, humor written all over his face. "Okay."

"Okay." She put her hands to the table, intending to push up and then get him to take her home. She only made it halfway before her muscles protested and she sank back to her chair. "Ouch," she said.

In a moment, Zane was up and on his knees beside her, shouldering Gambler out the way and shifting the chair so he could get his hands on one of her legs. Then long fingers began to massage the bare skin from mid-thigh to calf.

Heaven. She bit back a moan, caught between embarrassment and relief. "You don't need to do that."

"Would you rather I kiss it and make it better?"

"Not funny." She frowned at him, all the while biting back another moan. "I don't need any more kissing. I'm a runner now." It probably wouldn't make any sense to him.

Obviously not, because he wore another grin. "Since when are you a runner?"

"Since today, as you've probably figured out. The only thing I truly need now is the will to continue running so I'm in good enough shape to finish the mud run at the end of the month."

"I can help you with that," he said instantly.

"Huh?"

"I'll act as your trainer," Zane offered.

She stared. "Why would you?"

"To pay you back, Harper. You did me a favor at the diner the other night and while you might not fully understand it yet, the whole town believes we're a couple. Might as well take advantage of that and let me help you prepare for the mud run."

Panic fluttered in her belly. "Can't you tell the townspeople they're mistaken?"

He shook his head. "It doesn't work that way."

"We could have a big public break-up then," she said, brightening. "In the diner. You can loudly tell me that I'm not right for you. Too bookish."

"I couldn't do that. I like books."

Argh. He was so frustrating. She knew deliberately obtuse when she heard it. "Say I'm bland and boring then." They were Geoffrey's words, but she managed to get them out anyway. "They'll all believe it."

Zane's eyes narrowed. "If this is about leopards and dust bunnies again, I really will have to kiss you."

Holding up her hand, Harper pressed back in her

chair. "Please, Zane."

With one big palm on each knee, he studied her face, then sighed. "What am I going to do with you, Harper Grace?"

Before she could answer, he did so himself. "Be your trainer until the end of the month. As well as your friend."

Chapter 5

With Gambler leashed at his side, Zane strode up the path to the library entrance. It was a pleasing one-story building, nestled in trees, with dark gray-shingled siding, a deep porch, and double doors painted bright red. Around the back, he knew, was a patio with benches then a rolling stretch of grass that was often used by patrons in the summer.

Today, the cloudless sky promised that particular season might actually arrive soon. Zane took the blue overhead and the warmth of the sun on his shoulders as a good omen. There was going to be a way out of the corner he'd backed himself into with Harper.

He only needed to turn off his stupid switch.

It had been flipped to the On position one other time, when he was training in Fort Knox, Kentucky. A beautiful Southern belle had led him around by the nose for a time, and he'd been smitten by Lucy's soft drawl, her fancy high heels, even the way she complained about his big hands creasing her dress or messing with her hairstyle when they necked in her daddy's front parlor.

He'd bought her gifts he couldn't afford and arranged lavish dates that she'd seemed to enjoy—and think her due. Looking back, she hadn't so much played hard to get, but hard to get to know, and his dumb young self had been hooked by the feminine mystery of her, big time.

After an intense couple of months, knowing deployment was in the offing, he'd gone down on one knee with a ring in his hand.

That's when he found out that while he was good enough to date, to kiss, to accept presents from, he was also too big, too loud, and too rough for her to consider as husband material.

Really, she'd said, for *any* woman to consider husband material.

A lady wanted a gentleman who had a finer side.

Pushing away the unpleasant memory, Zane slid his hand into his pocket. The bookmark was there, that little thing he'd never quite managed to get back to Harper yet. But so was a tube of liniment.

A friend would provide that, because he guessed that today her muscles had to be stiff and sore.

Though he didn't know what he was going to do about that rash promise to be her trainer, which would mean way too much togetherness, today's friendly gesture he could make—and hope any second now his smart switch would flip.

As he and his dog reached the entrance, an older lady stepped out. He almost groaned aloud, but instead pasted on a smile. "Hi, Hildie."

The silver-haired woman lifted both arms in welcome, causing the sleeves of her striped caftan to flare out like bat wings. Gambler instantly dove between Zane's legs, his ninety pounds cowering there.

Add another item to the Terror List—Hildie's wacky wardrobe.

"Zane," she said now, completely ignoring the dog who was emitting tiny whines and hiding his face against his owner's jeans. "I've just met the pretty new librarian."

Yeah, and since she didn't have any books in hand, he figured Eagle Ridge's biggest gossip had gone into the building for just that very purpose.

Hildie Fontana owned and operated "Hildie's House," a pink cottage filled with white elephants—at least that's what the knickknacks and "antiques" appeared to be in Zane's eyes. Mostly she used it as a place from which she held court, dispensing chocolate chip cookies all day long as well as giving out and taking in the local gossip.

"I hear you and Harper are an item," Hildie continued.

He stifled another groan. "We're, uh, just friends."

The old woman tittered, as he'd known she would, proving true what he'd told Harper the day before—Eagle's Ridge had coupled them up and demurs and denials wouldn't do a lick of good.

Despite the fact that he was no good for the pretty new librarian.

"She seems very nice," Hildie said. "I think you'll do well together."

We broke up. The three words gathered on his tongue, prompted by the suggestion Harper had made the day before. But for the life of him, he couldn't push them out. Damn.

Hildie grasped her skirts in each hand and lifted her hem to continue on her way. "You should come by the shop, dear boy, I have a fresh batch of cookies in the jar."

"The last time I stopped in, I broke a vase and the chair I sat in collapsed underneath me."

She laughed. "Your handsome company's worth much more than a few broken things."

Touched, Zane turned to kiss her cheek as she passed. "Maybe you could be my girl."

On another little giggle, she pushed at his chest. "You've already got one of those," she said, her gaze shifting over his shoulder.

He turned back to see Harper standing in the open doorway, and his optimistic mood fled.

There was no cloudless sky, no sunshine on his shoulders.

Summer was a long, long way off.

Because looking at her, instantly feeling that pull she had over him, he knew he was stuck on stupid. Maybe indefinitely.

Today, she wore a soft sweater set, like girls from the 1950s or something, in a pale blue with pearl buttons. On the bottom was a full black skirt and little black flats. Her hair was pulled from her face and clipped at the back of her neck.

She looked proper and tidy and his hands itched to mess her up.

And not in a friendly sort of way.

Her hand lifted in a small wave. "Hi, Zane."

"Hey, buddy," he said, trying to look at her like a pal instead of like Gambler at a steak bone. "I, uh, brought you something."

Her head tilted. "A present for me?"

And screw him, how he wished he had flowers or candy or some little trinket for her, something to warrant that pleased expression on her face. "Yeah," he said gruffly, withdrawing the tube from his pocket. "Liniment for your muscles."

"Oh." Her pleased expression didn't drop. She moved forward, taking it from his hand.

"It's odorless," he said. "I wouldn't get you the stinky kind."

I wouldn't get you the stinky kind. Good God, could he sound more graceless?

But she beamed at him anyway. "That's nice of you. I did wake up a little sore this morning."

"Yeah, and it will only get worse until you go on another run."

"Good advice. I'll go out again tomorrow afternoon."

"There's a nice jogging trail in the park at the east end of Sentinel Bridge." He didn't offer to partner on that, and she didn't seem to notice.

Instead, her head remained bent over the liniment, so her eyes were hidden by her long, feathery lashes. "This is so sweet and thoughtful."

Nice. Sweet. Thoughtful.

Hell. She could not get the wrong idea about him. That just wouldn't do.

He gritted his teeth, then forced his jaw to relax. "Buddy."

She glanced up.

"Buddy," he said again. "I'm not sweet. Or nice. Or thoughtful."

Her head did that cute tilt again.

"I'm a guy. A rough-around-the-edges,

sometimes ill-mannered, belching kind of guy."

Her mouth pursed as if she was holding back a laugh. "I don't think you belch."

"I did when I was twelve. The entire alphabet." When she truly laughed this time, he gazed on her with some exasperation. "What I'm trying to say is…is…maybe I *am* a leopard. And leopards don't change their spots."

"Are you trying to tell me you could still burp the alphabet?"

"If I wanted to." And why that came out surly, he didn't know.

"Well, anyway, I have to get back to work," Harper said. Coming closer, close enough that he could smell the fragrance of her hair, she popped onto her tiptoes.

Her lips brushed his cheek.

And even at that delicate touch, lust surged. "Harper," he groaned, his hands flexing.

Then the distinctive whirr of a skateboard's wheels on asphalt sounded and Gambler, forgotten during his owner's conversation with the pretty, distracting, tempting librarian, bolted, his leash slipping from Zane's loosened hold.

"Gambler!" he yelled, lunging after the fleeing animal. "Gambler, get back here!"

The dog's scamper didn't slow as he rounded the corner of the library building.

"Oh, no," Harper called from behind him. They were both in hot pursuit now. "There are kids back there."

Bad. Very bad. Zane didn't think the canine would actually bite anyone, but he might easily knock a child over or scare someone into a stroke. Pumping his arms, he sped around the side of the library.

On the patio, on the grass. Kids.

Kids…and more dogs?

He stopped, his breath moving harshly in and out of his lungs, and stared. Harper came up beside him, she was panting too, but he didn't look at her.

The sight in front of him was impossible to look away from.

On a patch of grass, shaded by a tree, a little girl stood in pink tights, a pink-and-blue polka dot dress, with miniscule sneakers on her feet. And at them sat a very calm, very alert yellow Lab.

"Is that someone else's dog?" he wondered aloud.

"I think he's yours," Harper said, her voice low.

Zane began to move forward again, back in rescue mode, but she caught his arm. "Don't rush."

"What's going on?" he asked, glancing over at her.

"This is our Kids Reading to Dogs program," she whispered.

Of course it was, because about a dozen small kids sat about, with about an equal number of attentive canines beside them—though one kid had a rabbit in a basket. All the animals seemed content to be read to from the books in the children's hands.

"My predecessor started looking into it before she left, and I followed through with the idea. Studies show children's reading skills really improve when they have a non-judgmental ear."

Zane's gaze slid back to Gambler. He might be leaning against the little girl's legs now. "Maybe you should go get my dog. I might scare that kid."

He felt Harper's gaze on him. "You wouldn't scare a kid."

"I wouldn't mean to, but I often seem to anyway."

Shaking her head, the librarian moved past him and to a stack of books on a nearby table. After selecting a few, she moved toward the kid-Gambler pair. A small blanket was spread on the grass nearby.

Zane followed at a cautious distance, arriving in time to hear Harper say in her soft voice, "Bella, this is Gambler. Would you like to read him a book?"

Zane nearly lost his mind. Yeah, the dog might be having a moment of calm, but any second now his Zen could be broken by bubble wrap or a frog sighting. "Uh…" He put his hand on Harper's shoulder. "Do you think—"

"I think you should sit down right here, Zane, on the corner of the blanket so you can leave enough room for Bella and her reading partner."

The kid didn't say a word, but she did plop onto the blanket and Gambler instantly settled within reaching distance, his head on his front paws, his big browns trained on Bella's face. Without knowing what else to do, Zane took his own place as directed by the librarian.

And then he just watched. In amazement.

He didn't know what astounded him more, to see that the tiny kid could read, actually read—she couldn't be more than four or five, could she?—or that his undisciplined, unpredictable dog remained frozen in place, apparently listening.

It was as if Gambler had found his purpose.

Harper bent to whisper in his ear. "Bella's new to the program. This is her first time and she seemed very shy upon arrival. We also didn't have enough dogs to go around today, so this works out well."

Something involving Gambler was working out well!

Still dumbfounded, as Harper wandered away Zane remained in the shade of that tree and watched magic happen. The child's hand creeped out and as she read she began to pet the dog's head and play with his ears. The sight of those little fingers topped with pink glittery polish did something to Zane. Never one for keeping still for long, not since he'd won the battle with asthma anyway, now he found himself staying as motionless as his pet, unwilling to intrude by word or deed into the surprising interlude.

The girl's sweet small voice washed over him, and he and Gambler listened intently, still unmoving, even as she picked up a second book, and then a third.

Finally, a little bell rang and Zane came back to himself as if from a dream. Harper stood on the patio, all smiles. "Thank you for coming to today's program, boys and girls," she said. "If you want to go inside now, there's punch and cookies in the children's section and you'll meet your parents there. The dogs and the bunny will stay outside and be collected by their owners."

Kids began getting to their feet, including Bella, who stacked up the books she'd read and handed them to Zane. Then, to his bemusement, she kissed the top of Gambler's head and followed that up by sliding her tiny hand in his.

"Happy to make your acquaintance," she said, as polite as any mini-adult could be. "I'm Bella."

"Zane," he said, more bemused and equally beguiled.

She continued to hold his hand. "Could I read to your dog again someday?"

"He seems to like the way you tell a story," he answered, nodding.

Her face broke into a smile sure to slay hearts. Zane felt his own take a blow.

Then Harper was strolling toward them, a man at her heels. He didn't look at the other guy, because he could only see the librarian's face, the soft expression overcoming it as she took him in, Bella's hand still in his big paw.

God, the librarian was pretty.

And she wasn't looking at him like he was a big, loud, rough guy. No, she was looking at him like he was a hero.

Shit.

Still, whatever spell listening to Bella's voice had cast over him, the shine in Harper's eyes intensified it. The new calm settled more deeply over him and he felt his usual need to do, to move, ebb further away. He thought he could spend the rest of his life looking into the librarian's lovely face. His chest began to ache, like someone was prying open his ribs, except the hurt didn't exactly hurt, it—

"Leopards and spots," Harper murmured.

Killed. That look in her gray eyes was killing him.

"Bella," a male voice said.

Both the girl and Zane jerked their heads to the dark-haired man who'd halted just beside the librarian. Damn, if it wasn't another of his old friends come back to Eagle's Ridge. And though he was obviously fighting fit, Zane noticed right away that something heavy hung on the SEAL's broad shoulders.

"Uncle Noah!" Bella flung herself at him.

Noah stood frozen in her embrace, then his hand finally lifted to touch the child's silky hair. "I wasn't sure you'd recognize me."

The little girl stared up at him, her arms still wrapped around his waist. "We look at your picture every night. Mommy and me pray for you to come home safe."

A pained expression crossed Noah's face. "That's sweet of you. I think of you guys too."

"Are you home to stay?" Bella asked. "Mommy wants you back here with us."

"Right now I'm here to take you home to your mom. Did you, um, have a fun morning?"

Bella let go of her uncle in order to point at the dog. "I read to Gambler. He belongs to that man. That man is Zane."

"I know Zane." Still without a smile, Noah held out his hand. "Z, how are you?"

"I'm good." Better than my old friend, Zane thought. "When did you get into town?"

"Just today." He glanced over at his young relative, shadows in his eyes. "Today I'm helping out my cousin Lainey. This is her little girl."

"Ah," Zane said. He knew that Lainey was a widow and had been raised like a sister to Noah. Clearly something was up to bring the Navy SEAL back here from his DC digs. "And your cousin needs your help because…"

"Reasons why aren't great."

"Can we give you a reprieve from them this evening then?" Zane asked. "Can you get free to meet up at Baldie's tonight? We'll have beer and greasy bar food. Share some laughs."

At Noah's nod, Zane slid his phone from his

pocket. "Ryder's around. Adam, too. Wyatt as well. I'll text them right now. Six o'clock."

"Sounds good." The other man hauled in a breath and looked over at the little girl as if he wasn't quite sure what to do with her. "You ready to leave, Bella?"

She agreed, placing her hand into her uncle's. Zane gathered his dog's leash. "Gambler and I will walk you two out, if you don't mind going around the side of the library instead of straight through."

The pair proceeded to follow his plan, then Zane proved his stupid was still on, full-strength, because as they moved off, he looked back at Harper. She was flitting about the patio straightening up, like some kind of book fairy in that full skirt, little flats, pearl buttons.

Noah glanced that way too, then at Zane. A brief smile twitched the corners of his mouth, and for a moment he looked more like the teen Zane had spent so many hours with in high school detention. "View around Eagle's Ridge is improving."

It's my *view,* Zane thought.

But he stopped himself from claiming that aloud. Just barely.

Still, he chanced a second last look at her.

A breeze had come up, plastering her skirt to her thighs, delineating the lithe muscles he'd had his hands on the night before. He could feel her smooth, warm skin on his palms even now and couldn't believe he'd managed not to drag her to his floor, strip her completely bare, then sample all that proper and tidy and sweet, from the top of her head to her smallest toe.

Lingering, of course, in the hottest, wettest of places. Gorging himself on her scent and on her taste.

Because he really was a beast of sorts, a man with rough edges and with exhaustive appetites.

Appetites that might frighten her. That might overwhelm her.

That might break her.

So he had to figure out a way to keep her safe from all that he wanted from her, because as deep as that went, it wouldn't be what she needed and he didn't have anything more than right now and rowdy times to offer.

And everything about the pretty librarian still screamed forever.

Zane looked forward to a night with the guys. Spending time with his old friends and his brother without any distracting women around would remind him of exactly who he was—and what he couldn't be. Pushing open the door to Baldie's, a dimly lit roadhouse of a place that had neon beer signs on the walls and an impressive list of craft beers and a just as unimpressive list of call liquors, he breathed in the pleasing scents of spilled brew and a deep fryer at work.

Behind Baldie's bar no blender could be found, but you could order greasy chow from the kitchen guaranteed to forestall a morning-after hangover. The cheese fries were a locally known cure for the common cold.

As his eyes adjusted to the gloom, he noted that he was the first of his party to arrive. It made sense he was early, because he was that eager to kick back and just be Zane—uncomplicated in his tastes and his lifestyle. A man who operated a business and didn't get into other people's. A guy who'd talk all night about the team's chances for a play-off berth but didn't want to talk about anything deeper. Certainly not about anybody's feelings.

He strode inside, looking for a couple of tables to pull together, and saw his father seated at the bar. His posture, curved over his beer so low that his nose nearly dipped into the skim of foam at the top, didn't appear to be the pose of a man relaxing with a brew on a Saturday night.

Zane hesitated a second, then crossed to him on a sigh, taking the stool beside the older man. "Hey, Dad."

Sam looked over. "Son."

"I've got the dog in the family. And I happen to know he's at home, perfectly fine, presumably gnawing on the nylon bone I just bought him, or more likely, one of my shoes. So it can't be that."

His father's brows drew together. "Come again?"

"My dog's in good health, Dad, not run over, like your expression might lead other people to believe."

A half-smile lifted the corners of his dad's lips. Sam Tucker was a good-looking man, everyone said so, with his salt and pepper hair and chiseled features. But that smile didn't make it to his blue eyes tonight. "I'm fine."

Zane glanced around, first checking out the score of the game on the overhead TV. Nothing to be sad about there. The TV on the left wall showed a beer commercial that included several busty ladies, again not something to dampen his dad's mood. Then he looked to his right, and spied a lone woman at one of the tables.

Oh.

"Brenda's here," he said.

Sam slid his eyes in that direction and his face once more settled into a frown. "I saw her."

"Maybe you should join forces," Zane suggested. "You're not usually a drinking-alone kind of man."

"I don't know what I am," Sam muttered. "And I certainly don't know who Brenda is any longer."

Great. Zane cleared his throat. "Maybe you should, I don't know, go over there, get to know her again."

"I'm supposed to already know her!" Sam said, his voice heated. "I've known her longer than you've been alive!"

Zane winced. "Maybe you're a little unbalanced because of the news about Mom—"

"This has nothing to do with your mother," his father ground out. "Absolutely zilch."

Holding up both hands, Zane slid off his stool and onto his feet. "Okay, okay."

"I'm here to meet Pete," Sam continued. "But I saw Brenda, stopped to ask if she would like some company."

"Okay."

"She said no. She said she's meeting someone."

From the sour expression on his father's face, Zane assumed his dad thought she was meeting a man—one of those online daters most likely.

Sam's eyes narrowed. "And she said it in a very, very kind tone of voice."

"That witch," Zane said mildly.

"She's not been kind to me lately," Sam muttered, his gaze returning to his beer. "We do better when we're not talking."

Not going to touch that one, Zane thought. "Okay, well, Dad, I've got my own group to meet—"

"What the heck is going on?" Sam demanded. "Your sister finds a man, your brother finds a woman, Brenda's dating. Why can't things be like they used to be?"

Zane could sympathize, of course. "I know how you feel." The bar's door opened and Noah walked in. Zane lifted a hand, started in his direction, then leaned back toward Sam.

"If it makes it any better, Dad, I'm planning on being your crusty ol' bachelor son until the day I die. Ready and somewhat willing to spoon feed you and Grandpa Max porridge and strained peas for breakfast, lunch, and dinner."

At his father's reluctant chuckle, Zane left him to his beer and low mood.

He waved Noah to a table and put in for a pitcher of beer and some of those cheese fries with the server who bopped up. She was a cute thing, with dark hair cut short as a boy's but Zane's old friend glowered at her retreating form.

"How old do you think she is?" Noah asked.

"Uh, twenty-two? Twenty-three?"

"Bella's going to be twenty-two someday. But before that it's going to be years and years of pink ribbons and glitter pens and making sure some horny boy doesn't get in her head and mess with her chances to be the Secretary-General of the United Nations or the CEO of her own Fortune 500 company, or, best yet, the doctor who finds the final cure for cancer."

"Okay."

"She's really smart, Zane." His friend forked his hand through his hair. "Whip smart. That can't go to waste."

"Of course not," he murmured. And he'd seen for

himself the little girl's accelerated reading skills.

Conversation halted as the beer and the cheese fries were delivered. Neither seemed to improve his old friend's temperament. Zane took a long swallow of beer then found he couldn't stand the strained look on Noah's face any longer.

"What's wrong?" he asked.

"Lainey, man, she's like a sister to me."

"I know." Zane swallowed more beer.

"And she's really got no one else in the world but me." Noah pinched the bridge of his nose between his thumb and forefinger.

"Okay."

His friend hauled in a deep breath. "She's been diagnosed with cancer. The prognosis isn't good. It isn't good at all."

"Shit." Zane thought of cute little Bella, already fatherless. "I'm sorry. Is there anything I can do?"

"Noah shook his head. "I'm thinking about coming back. Returning to Eagle's Ridge for good."

"What the hell?" A new voice pushed into the discussion. Wyatt Chandler clapped Noah on the shoulder and then dropped into the chair beside him. "Did I just hear that? You're leaving your team?"

Noah bent his head, studied his beer. "There comes a time."

Wyatt's face closed down. "Yeah. Can't argue with that."

Then Noah shared with their other friend the situation he was facing. "Damn," Wyatt said, and poured himself a beer from the pitcher and nearly downed the thing in one glug. "So you're getting out."

"There comes a time," Noah repeated.

Hell, what it was time for, was to get this party

started, Zane thought, looking at his two glum buddies. Hadn't he promised they'd share some laughs?

Life could kick you in the teeth, that was sure, but tonight was supposed to be about letting go and having fun. For himself, Zane wanted to recall who he was before people in his family started going moon-eyed. Before his dog knocked over the local librarian and one look at her had knocked *Zane* off-kilter.

His attention turned from his friends as the door of Baldie's opened again. A couple of men entered together, but neither part of their expected group.

Zane glanced at his buddies. "What'll you bet my brother's the last of us to arrive and he'll have his cell to his ear, still talking to his woman when he walks in?"

Noah's gaze shot to Zane's. "Adam's got a woman?"

"He's whipped and wrapped."

For the first time, the other man's mouth stretched into a familiar grin that brought back old memories, old fun. "Last man in, phone to his ear, his woman on the other end, you say?"

"Ten bucks if I'm wrong."

Noah frowned. "You know I don't like to bet money."

Zane thought of the other man's prowess with everything mechanical and automotive. "Change my oil then, if I'm right."

"Done." They slapped palms on it.

Ten minutes later, the mood at the table had elevated. Ryder arrived, and then finally Adam, his phone to his ear as predicted. Zane snatched the device from his brother before he could sit down and said into it, "Jane?" His suspicions confirmed, he grinned. "It's Jane."

Noah shook his head. "Whipped and wrapped, who would have thought it?"

General, good-natured bull-shitting ensued after that. Then they talked about Wyatt's grandmother and Noah's new plan to return home—including the why of it.

That sobered the group again, but the SEAL was cheered when Adam mentioned that a local business, Nuts and Bolts Auto Repair, was for sale. It had been around for decades and serviced everything from farm trucks to Mercedes. The trusted shop could make a man a good living. Noah nodded, looking lighter by the minute.

Next they placed a call to Jack Carter, another member of their detention "club," and a former Marine. Now living in Seattle, Jack hadn't been back to town in who knew how long. He'd been expected to return for Founders' Day in March and had been a no show. Now his fellow detention detainees decided he needed to get some shit for being so out of touch.

As the phone was passed around, Zane half-listened to his buddies razzing their old friend and stretched out his legs and relaxed in his seat, for the first time in too long feeling comfortable in his life and in his own skin. So his sister and his brother went spinning off into true coupledom. Maybe his dad was having some sort of parallel mid-life crisis with the woman who was really more like a mom to Zane than the one he had. But he was now at Baldie's, beer and cheese fries making friendly in his belly and warding off germs, and all was right with his world.

He let his gaze roam the room skipping over his

dad now shoulder-to-shoulder with Pete. Zane's aim was to avoid Brenda, he didn't need a glimpse of her online dater, no way, but a flick of movement from that direction caught his eye.

His head jerked. His eyes narrowed on another table occupied by another woman. "She's over there having a drink," he said out loud. "At Baldie's of all low-life places."

It interrupted the flow of conversation that had started up after his buddies had ended the call with Jack. The others gathered around the table looked to Zane.

"This isn't a low-life place," Ryder protested. "I'm here."

"Too low-life for her," Zane muttered, ignoring the other man's joke and nodding in the direction of the table where Harper Grace sat, her long, dark honey hair swirling around her shoulders encased in that sweet, 1950s-style sweater. She'd exchanged the skirt for a pair of black, skinny-leg pants and instead of the flats, she wore high-heels, three inches of them, that had pointy toes and looked to be fashioned out of some black, snakeskin leather.

"Man, Miss Woody is still a looker," Wyatt said. "I can't get over it."

Zane blinked. Oh. Oh, yeah. Sitting across from Harper was none other than their former high school teacher.

Adam's lips twitched. "Zane's not looking at Miss Woody."

"Yeah?" Noah turned his head, took a gander. "Oh, the librarian. I thought there was something happening between you two today, Zane."

"Huh," Wyatt said. "She's not your usual type, Z.

You go for the good-time girls. She looks like just a good girl."

Zane glared at him. "We're only friends."

His brother snickered. "Really?"

We broke up. He thought of saying it, he really did, but like when he'd spoken to Hildie earlier in the day, the words wouldn't come out of his mouth.

Forcing his gaze away from Harper, he topped off his beer mug from the new pitcher they'd ordered.

"So, what else is new, Wyatt?" he asked. "You gotta line on that exciting new career you're after? Grizzly wrestling, wasn't it?"

His friend ignored the banter, his gaze elsewhere. "There goes Miss Woody. Over to the bar. Now Augie's got her cornered."

"Augie?" Adam craned his neck. "That suck-up. He drooled around her all through high school, cleaning her erasers and shit. He can't imagine he has a chance with her now, can he?"

Wyatt spoke up again. "Zane, your girl is alone. Looking a little uneasy."

Because she was better than this damn, low-life bar. But he wasn't going to look. He was going to stay right here and enjoy being Zane Tucker, Confirmed Bachelor Man.

Noah's attention had been snagged too. "Andy Smerkman, as I live and breathe."

Smerkman. The man kept turning up like a bad penny.

"Looks like he's clocked your girl," Noah said.

"*What?*"

"Yeah. He's starting to prowl in her direction. A total Smerkman move, by the way. Lone woman, new to town, Smerkman's moving in."

His jaw tight, Zane stared into his full beer. All remained right with his world, right here, damn it. With his buddies. Drinking brew.

"Bet you can't sit on your ass for the rest of that beer," Adam said, his voice sly.

"Sure I can." Without another thought, Zane downed the contents of his mug, slammed it on the table, and shot to his feet.

"Twenty says you'll wake up in that woman's— I'm sorry, your *friend's*—bed in the morning."

"Forty says I won't," Zane bit out, and then he was gone.

Chapter 6

Harper struggled against the urge to slide her book out of her purse or at least her phone. After all, part of being a new-and-improved Harper involved becoming comfortable with taking a meal alone, or even a drink. And Diana Woods, the woman who'd suggested they do so together, had merely excused herself to say hello to an acquaintance. Surely, she'd return soon.

So instead of burying her nose in her paperback or the e-reading app on her phone, Harper sat back in her chair and reflected on what she'd accomplished that day.

The Kids Reading to Dogs program had gone off without a hitch, despite, or maybe because of, Gambler's unexpected appearance. The uneven ratio of pets to children had made her fret for a few minutes until he'd raced to the patio and found a literacy partner in adorable Bella.

Watching the child read to the dog—and watching Zane Tucker watching the child read to the dog—had set off a flurry of warm tingles throughout Harper's body. The man expressed concern he might frighten the girl, but like the dog, he'd been perfectly well-behaved in her presence.

But Harper liked that he'd been worried. That said something. That said he was a good man.

Diana Woods had confirmed it for Harper. The stunning fortyish woman had introduced herself to the new librarian some weeks back, welcoming her to town and explaining she worked at the local high school. They'd had a couple of pleasant conversations since then. This evening, after locking the library, a car had pulled up to the curb as Harper began her walk home.

Diana Woods had smiled and suggested they go out for a beer or a glass of wine to further their acquaintance.

Being spontaneous and not letting her usually shy nature stop her from new experiences were both on her new-and-improved Harper to-do agenda. So she'd climbed into the passenger seat and after a brief stop at her condo to change some of her clothes, they'd taken a short journey.

Now here she was, at a bar called Baldie's, that was as far as a place could get from the San Francisco drinking establishments she'd been known to visit with Geoffrey or her girlfriends. A jukebox belted out classic rock, the drinks menu boasted only three wines—red, white, and rosé—and people were being served huge platters of fusion cuisine…basically cheese fused to potatoes.

She loved it.

Nursing her bottle of Stella Artois, chosen because it seemed a beer with a feminine-sounding name might be more her style than the others with the words "hairy" "dirty" and "dick" in their titles, she slid a look at a table across the room from under her lashes.

Zane. He sat with a group of big men about his age.

Diana had caught her gazing that way earlier.

I know all of those men. As teens, they filled up the desks during detention for an entire semester. Have you met any of them?

Harper had admitted an acquaintance with Zane.

Diana had admitted she'd already heard she and the man were an item.

He has a good heart under that rough exterior, though I don't think he's even completely aware of what's beneath all those rock-hard muscles.

All night, through the first beer and now this second, Harper had been completely aware of his every laugh, his every gesture.

Just as she was about to dare yet another peek, a man stepped to her table, blocking her view. Her chin tipped up.

"Hello," he said, smiling. His blond hair was cropped short and stiffened by gel. Unlike Zane, no hint of whisker grit edged his jaw. She could smell his aftershave even over the prevalent odors of beer and cheese-and-potato fusion.

"Um, hello." She glanced around to where she'd last seen Diana. The woman was still engrossed in conversation with a man with messy hair and egghead-style glasses.

The stranger's hand reached across Harper's table. "I'm Andy Smerkman."

Politeness necessitated her own hand come up to

meet his. But their palms had no chance to make contact because long fingers wrapped around her elbow and drew her instantly to her feet. "Hey, sweets."

Sweets. Zane Tucker stood beside her, wearing a pair of dark jeans and an ivory-colored, waffle-weave Henley that she'd been sneaking glances at all evening. Her gaze shifted from his broad chest to his face, noting again the five o-clock shadow around his mouth and along his jawline. His mesmerizing blue-green eyes were trained on her, as if the other man by her table didn't exist.

"Zane," said that other man now, his tone annoyed. "I'm right here."

"Me, too," he said, still without looking away from Harper. "And Harper and I have places to go."

Then he was hustling her out of the bar, forcing her to dig her heels into the sticky floor so she could scoop up her purse hanging over her chair. "I came with Diana."

Zane paused long enough to let out a short, sharp whistle. More than one person looked up, including Harper's drinks companion. He pointed to Harper, then at his chest, then jerked his thumb in the direction of the door.

With a smile, Diana nodded she understood the pantomime and sketched a small wave.

Zane began moving again, forcing Harper to tottle after him to keep up with his long strides. His hand remained curled around her arm and she tried breaking free, but he wasn't having it. And because of the tottle, she gave up, thinking she'd be more embarrassed on her way out the door if she fell on her behind before getting there.

Once in the chilly evening air, he led her in the direction of his truck.

"What if I have my own car?" she said, trying once again to halt his forward momentum.

"Do you have your own car?" When she didn't answer, he began tugging her again, pulling her around his back bumper to the passenger side of his vehicle.

There, he pushed her against the door and just stared down at her, exasperation written on every line of his handsome face. "What am I going to do with you, Harper Grace?"

He'd asked that once before. She opened her mouth.

But before words could escape it, his own mouth was there, his tongue sliding deep as one big, rough palm tunneled beneath her hair to curl around her nape. That raspy touch felt so good her knees melted, but it didn't feel nearly as good as his tongue sliding over hers, exploring everywhere. Then his lips left hers, but only to wander across her cheek where they touched the outer shell of her ear.

His hot breath dispatched cold chills down her neck and across her chest. Her nipples tightened to instant, painful points and her hands clutched at his biceps.

Then his head came up and he gave her another exasperated look. "Damn it. Now we're going to have to talk about *that* kiss," he said, as if it was all her fault.

Her temper kindled, but it was such an unusual sensation that it distracted her long enough for the man to bundle her into the passenger seat. Then he was behind the wheel and they were heading out of the Baldie's lot.

Despite the cold night, Harper felt hot under the collar, felt hot *everywhere*.

And the tension inside the cab of the truck was thick and heavy and made her skin prickle on top of the heat already there.

Due to all that, it took her a while to realize he wasn't heading directly to her condo. She frowned, trying to get her bearings in the dark. "Where are we going?"

He slowed, pointing out the building she knew was to house his sister Bailey's new restaurant. "That's my sister's place, the one she's opening in a short while."

"Okay." Harper peered at the stone building and continued looking at it over her shoulder as they drove on, lights illuminating the sign that said "Coming Soon—Blue Moon" receding in the distance.

"This is the diner, of course," he said a few minutes later, braking again. "No alcohol is served there, which keeps the atmosphere usually well south of raucous, but sometimes hunters come in after a morning of keeping warm with whiskey and begin to argue over the bullshit that hunters argue over. Occasionally the wait staff is forced to call in Dad or Brenda."

Her bewilderment grew. "Um, why are you telling me this?"

"I'm telling you that Dad and Brenda can handle things if you run into trouble at the diner, but most everywhere else you need to keep your eye out for unruly tourists and ill-mannered local mountain men. You're safe at the library and at your condo too. Then there's the Broadleaf—that upscale hotel in the middle of town—it has a quiet atmosphere and a sweet little bar called Sunfish. Diana should have taken you there."

"I like Baldie's. I like potato cheese fusion food."

He cast her an odd glance. "It's cheese fries."

"Same thing." She lifted a shoulder. "And I would be happy to go back there again. *You* were there. Your friends look nice."

"My friends are nice." He paused. "But not nice for you. And definitely Smerkman—who is not a friend—is not nice for you."

Harper crossed her arms over his chest as Zane hit the accelerator again. "I don't need a keeper."

"A woman like you needs to know the right places for a woman like you to go."

Her temper bubbled. "Oh, I get it. The sweet places, the quiet places, the safe places."

He pulled into her condo complex, and turned into a visitor's space.

"The *boring* places."

"Bailey's restaurant won't be boring," he said, his voice mild. He exited out of his side and came around to meet her as she jumped off the high passenger seat. When she teetered on her heels, he reached out both hands to steady her at her waist.

"But it's also the restaurant of a French-trained chef. So it's likely to be very proper, and, again, quiet." Harper turned away from him and began to march toward her unit. "Perfect for a boring person like me."

Without speaking, he trailed her to her unit, waiting while she unlocked the door. Then he pushed it open and followed her inside, swinging it shut behind him.

The living room was dimly lit, the timer having taken care of flipping on the lamp in the big picture window once it turned dark. The space was small but she'd decorated with light-colored walls and furniture upholstered in bright paisleys. To her eye, it was homey but not homespun. But Zane didn't seem to be admiring it, or even actually absorbing his surroundings, because he was staring at her.

"What is this about you being a boring person?" he finally demanded, as if he found that annoying.

When it was she who was annoyed.

"It's what my ex said about me when he broke our engagement," she informed Zane. "After two years of being my fiancé. After six months of him cheating on me with various one-night stands. On the very day I put down the deposit on the wedding venue."

Zane swore beneath his breath.

Now Harper put one hand on her hip, a pose she never thought she'd struck in her life. "But you know what? I don't think it's me that's boring. It's those kid gloves people like you put on when they get a look at me. Then they're telling me the places I should visit are only the safe and sweet places. *That's* the problem. The truth is, it's people like you who *make* me boring!"

He only continued to stare.

So she added, just to be honest, "Well, it's only mostly people like you to blame. Because I am a little shy. I grew up with my head in books. I'm always making up stories."

Now Zane looked like he was fighting a smile.

It caused her to glare at him. "But I might have been exciting if I was ever asked to do exciting things!"

"I'll take you kayaking," Zane said quickly. "Rafting too. Get you up on a paddle board and—"

"Not good enough." She leaned toward him, her temper still running hot. "To be exciting, I have to do exciting things in bed, too. That's also what Geoffrey told me."

Zane's eyes narrowed. "Geoffrey's an ass."

"Who has exciting times in bed." Now it seemed completely unfair that the new-and-improved Harper hadn't yet had new-and-improved sex. She half-wondered if this idea came from the two Stellas she'd downed in quick succession. It seemed a notion that a "Stella" might have. In any case, it deserved addressing.

"Why don't I get exciting times in bed?" she demanded from the only other person in the room.

Zane's chest started moving up and down, as if it was difficult for him to draw in air. "I don't know exactly how to answer that," he finally choked out. "And maybe this isn't the time."

"Oh, that's right, you had something else you wanted to talk about." Harper rolled her eyes, something her sister did often, but that she'd never much taken to before. It felt good, though. Expressive. "That last kiss."

Somehow Zane had moved nearer without her noticing. His broad chest was only an inch or so from her and one of his boots was wedged between her high heels. She'd noticed his size before—who couldn't notice his size, all that delicious, manly expanse of muscle?—but he seemed to expand before her eyes now.

Miles of hard planes and long bones and those

blue, blue eyes with their searing touch of green.

Now Harper couldn't breathe, and barely hear with the pounding of her heart sounding so loud in her ears. With widening eyes, she watched his hand come up, and then sift through her hair to once again cup her nape. To once again thrill her with the rough sensation of his callused palm against her softer skin.

"I don't think now's the time to talk about that last kiss," Zane said, his voice low. The sensual look in his eyes was making her shiver. "I think we have to go directly to talking about the next one."

Oh, God. Another quiver shook her body.

But she wasn't backing down—because it wasn't exactly fear, or all fear, that was causing these trembles. "Talk," she scoffed on another eye-roll, trying to sound brave. "Don't you get it? I want action."

"Action."

At that one, nearly growled word, she shifted her gaze to Zane's amazing eyes again. They'd gone even more intense. Hot. Burning.

Oh, wow.

Her womb clenched, her thighs trembled, a flush of heat washed over her skin.

"Yes," she said, tilting up her chin. "I want *action.*"

Zane felt Harper's body vibrating in his hold and it only served to ratchet up the heated lust pulsing through his veins. Hell, who knew how, but the sweet woman could bring out the down-and-dirty in him.

He tried to rein in the burn, though, gentling his hold on the back of her neck and lifting his free hand to caress her cheek with his thumb instead of finding the nearest bed ASAP. Her skin flushed under his touch.

"I think I know some of the problem," he said, staring into her upturned face. So. Damn. Pretty. "It's your name. Your first is a last name. Your last name is a first name. It's messed you up—makes you do things backward."

He saw her swallow. "How so?"

"You coupled yourself to someone then expected exciting times in bed. You should have experienced exciting times in bed with someone before even considering coupling yourself up with him."

Her small pink tongue darted out to moisten her bottom lip, and his cock went from hard to *hard*. "People think you and I are a couple," she said, her voice breathless.

"Yeah." He read where this was leading and he didn't think he had it in him to turn them back from this path. Not with that shy-but-needy librarian practically demanding "action" from him.

"Then I think I'm still doing it wrong," Harper said.

Yeah, demanding action. What man could resist? Certainly Zane knew it was impossible for *him* to resist her.

"You want to right that, honey?" He couldn't stop from asking the question as the edge of his thumb traced the apple of her cheek.

She took in a breath. "Yes, I want to right that, Zane." Her tongue made a reappearance, moist and pink, and he bent to capture it before it touched her lower lip.

He sipped it into his mouth, felt her jerk of reaction, felt his cock jerk too, trying to get out of his tight jeans and into her wet heat. His hands clutched, one at her neck, the other on her shoulder, his intentions instantly honed to one—seeking a bed, caveman-style, with Harper over his shoulder.

Then conscience intruded. No, he told himself, loosening his fingers and sliding them to either side of her waist. He could not turn rutting beast with the librarian. He could not show himself as one of those ill-mannered local mountain men he'd warned her away from.

Lifting his head, he stared down into her dazed eyes. "You want to take me to your room?"

She nodded, then he dropped his hands so she could turn and lead the way.

Though his cock thrummed with the solid beat of his heart, he managed to stroll behind Harper as she guided him into a spacious bedroom that smelled faintly of citrus blossoms. She'd be lost alone on the big mattress set at an angle in the corner, but it would fit the two of them just fine. Lamps on flanking bedside tables glowed at the flip of a switch and he saw that one held a stack of books and the other a chunky, unlit candle the size of a grapefruit.

He arrowed for it. "Matches?"

"In the drawer below," she said, and watched silently as he set flame to the three centered wicks.

The sweet, delicate scent wafted into the room as he crossed back to the switch and doused the lamps. He glanced at Harper, the candlelight flickering across her face.

"Nervous?" he whispered, again shutting down his urge to grab and plunder.

Her head shook slowly from side to side as he prowled nearer. "Ready."

"Not in all those clothes you aren't." Her hands instantly lifted to her top pearl button, but he brushed them away. "That's for me."

Unable to help himself, he bent to her face. "This is all for me," he said against her mouth.

As they kissed, he stripped her of the cardigan. The sweater shell went next, he whipped it over her head then returned to kissing, her smooth shoulders beneath his hands. She didn't seem to know what to do with hers. They fluttered at his biceps, moved to his waist, went back to his upper arms.

So he took her wrists and drew her arms around his neck. Her hold tightened there and he slanted his head to deepen the kiss as he unfastened and unzipped her pants. The fabric pooled at her ankles, and that's when he stopped kissing and started looking.

His head lifted and his breath stuttered in his lungs. She wore a matching bra and panties—of course Harper Grace wore a matching bra and panties—and they were of an ivory lace so close to the color of her skin it was nearly as if she wore nothing. But it was almost better than nothing, because he could see the jut of her rosy nipples through the bra cup and the panties molded her so closely that he could make out the contours of her sex.

Before the top of his head could blow off, Zane put pressure on her shoulders, pushing her to a sitting position on the end of the bed. Then he knelt on the rug at her feet, removing the snakeskin pumps to slide the pants away then popped the shoes back on her small feet.

Lust punched through his bloodstream as he sat back and allowed himself another look at Harper. Creamy skin, lacy underclothes, those high heels.

It felt as if one of them had pierced his heart.

"Lie back on your elbows, pretty thing," he said, feeling saliva gather in his mouth. He yanked her ass to the very edge of the mattress. "I've got something I need to do and you're going to want to watch."

Then he kneed closer, spreading her thighs to make room for his shoulders. Out of the corner of his eye, he saw her fingers dig into the coverlet as he buried his face in the heat of her, in the scent of female, in the heart of what he wanted more than his next breath.

She moaned, her hips lifting as he tongued her, wetting that lace until he could wiggle into the folds and find the bundle of nerves. She twitched, and fell back against the bed, one arm flung over her eyes. Zane lifted his head.

"Don't hide from exciting, little darling. Feel it. Let me hear it. Let me know you know how much I'm enjoying myself." He slid one finger under the elastic at her inner thigh, and let it skim her slippery wetness until he found her flowered opening and could ease his longest finger inside.

She clenched down on the intrusion, her moan sweet, low, and long.

His heart lurched. His cock protested the uncomfortable confines of denim. "That's it, pretty thing," he said, ignoring the sensations, as he slid in and out of her tight, hot channel. "Feel it. Feel everything."

Need burned in his veins. "Up on your elbows, Harper," he ordered now. "You don't want to miss this."

When she obeyed, he caught her gaze with his, then lowered his head to place a kiss on her belly just above the panty elastic crossing her hip. Then he caught it in his teeth, drawing it down without stopping the in-and-out movement of his finger.

The catch of her breath was loud in the room as he began to bare her. The panties stalled, and he tugged with his free hand so they cleared the curve of her ass. Then the scrap of material caught on his wrist, the lace brushing the inside of her thighs as he continued to slide in and out of her.

He stared down at her beautiful petals, her intimate flesh swollen and glistening with her arousal in the candlelight. A shudder worked its way down his back and around to his dick, which made its hunger known by releasing a hot spurt of pre-cum.

Then, on a groan, Zane lowered his head and fed the craving.

Harper cried out, more sweet and low, and he did work, man work, the best kind of work, tonguing and sipping and nipping and sucking. Her hips lifted to him, her wetness spreading on his lips and cheeks and chin and he felt the tension gather in her thighs that were clasped around his shoulders. He redoubled his efforts, the flat of his tongue on her hard clit then the slightest edge of his teeth.

She cried out again, louder this time. Sensing the crisis upon her, he sucked in that bundle of nerves and carefully inserted another finger inside her. Harper gasped, froze, clamped down on his possessive hand, and then—God, *beautiful*—came.

He pressed kisses to her belly as he waited for her tension to abate. When her inner muscles relaxed, he withdrew his fingers, let her panties fall to the floor, and climbed onto the bed, only to immediately crawl up her body in the direction of the neglected part of her he was about to pay attention to next.

"I'm a breast man," he said, undoing the clasp of her bra. "Well, to be honest, I'm an every- erogenous zone man." His head bent to kiss a suddenly freed nipple when a small hand pushed back on his forehead.

"You'll be a dead man if you don't get out of all your clothes," Harper declared.

Quite forcefully, it must be said.

Bemused, he sat up, straddling her nakedness and sent her a quizzical glance.

"Take them off, I said."

He felt his smile grow, even with his raging hard-on. It was impossible not to smile looking down at all her creamy nakedness and that set expression to her swollen mouth. "Your turn to play," he said obligingly, and tossed off his clothes.

Then she was up and on him, shoving his back to the mattress. He laughed, low and dirty, as his hand trailed her spine to her ass. He froze, then lifted his head and craned his neck to peer around her hip.

"Harper Grace," he said, taking in the lush, luscious curves of her butt. "You've been hiding that from me under those long sweaters, and I'm a definite ass man."

She pushed his shoulders back down and cruised her mouth across his collarbone. "Call me Stella."

"What?"

"When I'm going for exciting in bed I've decided I want to be called Stella."

He laughed, the sound cut off when she found his nipple and gave it a sharp little suck. He groaned, palmed her ass again, and gave it a light slap. "Whatever you say, Stella."

It turned out that Stella/Harper used her mouth for more important things than talking. She took it on a trip all over his chest, delivering peppery kisses, sucking kisses, the kind of kisses that drove a man mad. Then she attacked his mouth, taking the lead on even more kisses, as her hand traveled toward his groin.

Her fingers curled around his shaft.

Zane groaned into her mouth, his hips lifting, more pre-cum oozing. She found it with her thumb, wetting the head and making him crazy. "Do you have a condom?" she whispered against his mouth.

"Yeah." He panted instead of losing it, reaching a blind hand for the foil packet he'd placed on her bedside table. The books sailed off the surface because of his clumsy searching but then she had the foil and he watched, fascinated, as her small fingers tried to peel it open. Snatching it from her, he tore it with his teeth and rolled the thing on himself, his patience wearing thin.

Finally, she crawled on top of him. He steadied her with one hand, then helped her lower. "I've got myself a cowgirl," he said, grinning and groaning at the same time as her hot, tight flesh closed over him.

"Cowgirl Stella," she said, as if testing it out, and then she was riding him, taking him to a heavenly rodeo.

He gritted his teeth and merely accepted what she gave, trying to hold out as long as he could. But then it was impossible—he couldn't check himself any longer. So he lifted his head, found one sweet, pouty nipple, and drew it into his mouth. Hard.

She froze, then began to move again, grinding herself onto the root of his cock. "Touch yourself,"

Zane said, releasing her nipple. "Touch yourself, Stella."

And at the sound of her new name, the librarian slid her hand down her belly and found the right spot. Or so he figured, because her inner muscles began to spasm, her head dropped back, and her orgasm triggered his. His hips jerked, short thrusts that tumbled him over the edge of heaven and into the wide and wonderful pleasure fields below.

Later, coming back from the bathroom where he'd ditched the used condom and washed up, he found that Stella had turned to Harper again because she'd crawled between the covers dressed in a nightgown. The sheer cotton of it wrapped the part of her shoulder where the sheet left off. The candle still flickered, lighting her sleeping face.

He smiled and resisted the urge to wake her for a round two. That could wait.

Snagging his boxers from the floor, he glanced at the bed again. She'd pulled back the covers on the other side as well, a clear invitation. That didn't need to be made twice. He'd roll in there beside her, get some shut-eye, and in the morning he'd show his good manners and his gratitude by rocking Harper's— Stella's, whatever—world once more.

She'd find it was going to be even more exciting when he could play with all her pretty curves in the light of day. Into this moment of delightful anticipation, his twin's voice intruded.

Twenty says you'll wake up in that woman's—I'm sorry, your friend's—*bed in the morning.*

Damn it.

Zane couldn't stay, right? If he did, he'd owe his brother forty—he'd upped the ante himself—and there was no reneging on bets. Then the other guys who'd been at Baldie's with them would be sure to find out—not a one of them would have the decency not to pry, not when it meant foregoing a chance to rib a friend about a wager, won or lost.

But Zane didn't want them talking about Harper. He didn't want them picturing Harper in bed.

Quickly donning his clothes, he crossed on stocking feet to the candle and blew out the flames. Then he high-tailed it to her kitchen where he found a scrap of paper and a pen. Unsure exactly what to say, he scrawled a thanks and headed for the front door.

He eased it open and glanced right then left. If anyone saw him slipping out, they'd certainly guess what he'd been up to with her just by looking at him. He didn't need to confirm for anyone that Mr. Rowdy Fun and Right Now had been up close and intimate with the new librarian.

Chapter 7

Early Sunday morning Zane sat in his desk chair at A To Z, scrolling through the schedule and trying to focus on the day ahead instead of whom he'd been with the night before, when Adam strolled into the office. He set a coffee beside the computer and then wiggled two twenties in front of Zane's face.

Damn.

Snatching the bills, he half-shoved them under the pen- and pencil-filled cube on the desk.

"No wonder you look like hell," his twin said. "Blue balls, huh?"

"We shouldn't have made that bet," he muttered.

Adam fell back on one foot, his hand over his heart like he was having an attack. "You never hesitate to make a bet, take a bet."

"I shouldn't have done it this time." Only jerks bet on bedding woman, though he had bet that he would not. No difference.

"But—"

"Shouldn't have done it," Zane repeated, aware he sounded surly as hell.

"It wasn't exactly a land giveaway," Adam said.

That had been the seed for five decades of feuding that had divided the town. A card hand and a bet gone wrong…meaning that Grandpa Max had lost a tract of his most valuable land and winner John Westbrook hadn't hesitated to scoop it up. But there'd been other causes and other grudges that kept the hostility alive for years until Bailey and Ryder's romance forced everybody on both sides to begin to play nice, finally, just this spring.

At that moment, Gambler ambled into the office, took one look at the low cupboard door Zane had left open when he went for printer paper and nearly jumped out of his fur coat. With a whimper, he dashed to the knee well cut into the desk, knocking over a waste basket on his way, and cowered between Zane's legs.

His brother bent to peer inside the cabinet. "Better add boxes of paperclips to the Terror List."

Zane sighed, his hand reaching down to fondle the dog's ears. Just yesterday Gambler had seemed to be a whole new canine when listening to little Bella read. But there it was, proof that leopards didn't change their spots.

Adam hitched his hip onto a corner of the desk. "You know, we haven't talked about Wednesday night."

"Huh?" Zane gave his brother a wary look. He'd kissed the librarian in public on the sidewalk then. "What about Wednesday night?"

"When Bailey shared with us that Mom is coming back to town for her restaurant opening."

"Oh." Zane frowned. "That."

"I guess they're making a reunion movie for Mom's old sitcom."

"You mean Tori Remington's old sitcom." Their mother left for Hollywood as Vicky Tucker, but when she'd been cast as the mother in *Mother May I*, she'd become another person. Leaving her real name behind as well as her husband, sons, and daughter.

"According to Bailey, it got her thinking she wanted a chance to reunite with us."

"Huh." Zane returned his attention to his computer screen.

After a moment's silence, he sensed his twin's impatience. "Well?" Adam finally said. "What do you think about it?"

"That's my favorite part about being a twin. We know what each other's thinking most of the time, meaning we don't have to get into it."

"So then I'm right and you think it's crap that she's coming back because it might upset everybody—including threatening that he-man, got-no-soft-side front you show to the world—and you feel—"

"The two of us definitely don't get into our feelings," Zane hastily put in.

"Brother." Adam shook his head. "For God's sake, just because you don't like to talk about your feelings doesn't mean I believe for a second you don't have any."

Zane's head shot up and he pointed an accusing finger at his twin. "That woman has done something to you."

A small smile turned up his brother's lips. "That woman is Jane and you know you like her. *I* know you like her."

"Yeah, yeah," Zane said, conceding the point with little grace.

Adam remained looking amused. "And now that we're on that subject of females...what's up with you and the librarian?"

Zane would have liked to say it was none of his twin's business, but the fact was...twin. It came with the territory that he had to string a few words together to make an answer that filled in what his brother hadn't already intuited. Zane sighed. Opened his mouth.

And realized he didn't know what the hell to say.

Because he didn't know exactly what was up with him and the librarian. He wanted to say nothing was up, or at the very least, only that they were friends, but they'd had sex last night and then he'd left her to wake up alone. That wasn't nothing. Nor was it particularly friendly.

And it meant what he really didn't know was, what was up with Harper this morning. How she might be feeling now about...just, well, anything. Everything.

Hell. *Feelings* again.

Something had to be done. There was no doubt about it.

He squeezed shut his eyes then opened them to return his attention to the computer screen and the day's schedule. "I'm slated for a kayaking class at three," he said.

"I've got it covered for you," his brother replied. "No problem."

Proving the twin thing. Zane didn't have to even ask. His brother understood without words being spoken that he'd just assigned himself a pressing task.

Just as Zane understood that he couldn't get the woman out of his head until they had a short talk and came to a mutual grasp of what last night had meant…and what it didn't mean for the future.

In that, there was no future for the two of them.

To make that happen, at around 3:30 he was skulking at the park trying hard not to look as if he was skulking at the park. He had running shoes on his feet, workout pants and a T-shirt covering the rest of him, Gambler on the end of a leash. It was only speculation that she'd come to run here as he'd suggested, but as everyone knew, he was a gambling man.

Which this time, as it so often did, paid off.

Earbuds in her ear, her attention on the phone in her hand, Harper came jogging along the trail, wearing navy-blue running tights and a matching jacket. Her hair, worn in a high ponytail, swung side-to-side with each step.

He stood on the edge of the path, Gambler pressed to his knees. When Harper registered Zane's presence, he saw her jolt. Her feet halted and her gaze jumped to his.

"Hey, Harper," he said.

"Hey," she returned, in that toneless, almost-too loud voice people used when their ears were plugged.

Reaching out, he snagged the pink cord and popped out one of the devices. "Care for some company?"

"Um…" Her glance returned to her phone, but it didn't hide the flush that was crawling up her cheeks. "I've got an audio book to pass the time."

He put the bud to his own ear, listened, then

grimaced. "Someone is getting brutally murdered. I must be better company than that."

Gambler chose that moment to leap at Harper. Zane managed to rein him in, but instead of exhibiting panic, she laughed at the dog and bent over to pet him. "I've got your number, you big, silly softie," she said, kissing the dog's head. "You're no threat to me at all."

"So you'll let us run with you?"

Instead of answering, she retrieved her earbud from Zane, bundled the cord, and stuffed it and the phone into the pocket of her stretchy hoodie. Then she glanced at him, as if having second and third thoughts.

"If you start lagging," he said, "I promise Gambler and I will go all Butcher of Eagle's Ridge on you."

It made her laugh again, and then without another word she started off, nice and easy.

He thought it said something that she hadn't flat-out refused him, so he kept to her pace in silence for a few minutes. But more needed to be communicated.

"How are you?" he asked.

"Great," she replied, not yet breathless.

Zane searched his mind for the best way to bring up matters. It was mostly a first for him. Women he bedded knew him, knew the score. Spelling out that what they'd done didn't signal a relationship or a future—God, not that—had never been an issue.

He mentally tried out a couple of conversation-starters.

That was fun, but you have to know…

I really enjoyed myself, however…

He opened his mouth, hoping something along those lines would fall out. But instead, he heard himself ask, "Geoffrey?"

She glanced over. Wisps of dark honey hair had already worked its way free of her thick ponytail and fell around her face. Her small hand brushed them back.

So damn pretty, he thought, distracted from his own question.

"Geoffrey?"

The ugly ex. "How the hell did you get near-hitched to some dumbass cheater?" Zane demanded, startling himself with the heat in his voice. "Did you love him?"

Another glance, this one accompanied by a glare. "Of course not."

"Then why were you engaged to him?"

"Our mothers introduced us. They serve on a couple of charity committees together."

Cold washed over Zane.

"You're a society girl," he said, feeling stupid that he hadn't realized it sooner. Hadn't he been down this road before? She was the kind of woman who wanted—

"He's a corporate attorney."

Yep, Zane was right. She was the kind of woman whose people wanted her to marry an attorney, and not one that worked for truth and justice out of some cramped, dusty office, but a corporate type who worked to make a shit ton of cash and find a high perch in the great ladder of life.

Her people, just like Lucy's, would see Zane as the opposite of that. He wasn't even a Ryder Westbrook, the golden boy from the moneyed side of Eagle's Ridge. He was an ex-soldier, a man who had calluses and not papercuts on his hands. A man who wanted to spend his life on the river and in the mountains as opposed to wasting time in ballrooms and corporate retreats.

They wouldn't think him good enough for Harper.

They'd expect her to be with a *gentleman*.

Like the one who'd cheated on her.

"Did you love him?" Zane demanded again.

"No. I told you."

"So then—"

"I couldn't love a man who would do that, step out on me over and over with a succession of women. So whoever I thought I fell in love with…it wasn't Geoffrey."

"Just like the Butcher of Eagle's Ridge." Now Zane got it. "You made up in your head the Prince Charming of Harper Grace's life."

"I hope I wasn't that dumb," she said. "But I was dumb enough not to realize that a man shouldn't say he doesn't care about setting a wedding date. He shouldn't say that his fiancée should go ahead and do that whenever."

Whenever. Shithead.

"A man who really wants to marry someone should want to settle on a date right away."

Yeah. Zane couldn't imagine Ryder or Adam, once they popped the question, letting that detail go unresolved. Certainly not for as long as *two years*.

"So because I was that dumb or naïve or whatever you want to call it, he got to live his life, making his mother happy with an engagement to the right woman, without foregoing his exciting succession of one-night stands."

How Zane detested the jerk, he thought, fuming. And yeah, it didn't escape him that he'd experienced his own single-night flings, but he'd never been promised to marry anyone either.

The trail turned right and their footsteps thumped over a footbridge that crossed a narrow creek. Suddenly, there came a soft splash. Gambler yanked on the leash just as Zane saw a fat frog leap from the water and onto the bank. Lost in a mood over Harper and this Geoffrey character, Zane was unprepared for the dog's abrupt bolt and the lead slipped from his hold.

The Lab fled, going off-path and through the trees. Zane followed, of course, cursing and panting and sliding on wet leaves and patches of mud. Finally, executing a mad leg lunge, he managed to get his shoe on the trailing end of the leash. But then his sole slipped on more mud and he went flying up, only to land on his back in a graceless heap of pissed-off man.

Next Harper skidded up, just as Gambler turned around and rushed back to hover over his owner like he was a loyal canine overcome with concern and not a crazy, gigantic ball of fur with an absurd fear of amphibians. On a frustrated sigh, Zane struggled to a sitting position.

Female laughter rang through the trees.

He glanced up. Harper stood over him, her hands on her hips, her face alight with amusement. "You should have seen…" she said, then broke off to laugh some more. "That was q-quite the fall."

He tried quelling her with a glare, but found himself reluctantly laughing too, despite the ache in his bones. "Don't ever say I don't know how to show a woman a good time."

"I would never say that," she said, then with one small finger made a cross over her heart. She was still grinning.

And something shifted inside Zane. Maybe it was the limb-jarring fall. Or her expression. Or her eyes, their arresting gray trained on him and still alight with humor.

"I showed you a good time," he said.

Her face sobered. She knew he didn't mean just now.

"What we did was exciting," Zane continued. "Last night."

"Um…" She bit her bottom lip, her natural flush from the exercise turning to a much brighter pink. "Yes."

"I don't want to be tit," Zane declared, because that was the damn truth.

Harper blinked. "Um…what?"

"For tat." He got to his feet, his gaze focused on her. "I don't want to be a tit for tat."

Harper was all big eyes and now-moistened lips. "What do you mean?"

"What we had…it wasn't a one-night stand." Though that was exactly what he'd thought to make clear when he sought her out this afternoon. But his intention had shifted, for whatever reasons he chose not to examine at the moment. "I don't want to be payback to your cheating ex."

As if he'd slapped her, she jerked. "Zane…"

"It wasn't a one-night stand," he said, firmly.

Her hands flew to her hips and she pressed those moist lips together. "You don't have to try to save my pride. Maybe I *was* dumb and naïve then but don't think I am now. Just because we were together last night, I don't expect—"

"Yeah." He didn't expect either. He didn't expect

to be so certain about this. But the fact was, he didn't want to walk away like he had so many times before. Not from Harper. Not yet. "You can have a say in this, of course, but I'd like to see you again."

Her head tilted. "For another…run?"

He knew what that question meant. And it pissed him off that he'd made her feel like someone he only wanted to take to bed. But he couldn't blame her, could he? Yet he wanted to make clear he wasn't hoping to set her up as some sort of regular booty call.

He slowly bent for Gambler's leash, then straightened again and pinned her gaze with his.

"I want to take you to dinner," he said. "Tomorrow night."

Not two years from now. Not effing two *days* from now.

Her mouth dropped in surprise.

He held his breath.

And when she said "yes," Zane wasn't sure which of the pair of them was more surprised. Or pleased.

Or worried as hell, because this was new territory and he couldn't figure out what he thought or felt about anything. Damn. Feelings again.

Brother, for God's sake, just because you don't like to talk about your feelings doesn't mean I believe for a second you don't have any.

Harper had the day off and she had an emergency.

She didn't know how to get out of a date gracefully. Especially one that in her heart of hearts she wanted to go on more than anything.

This dilemma required coffee and the kind of breakfast served at No Man's Land.

So she took a brisk walk there from her condo, ignoring the muscle twinges from her second training run, and peered through the diner front windows. It was past the usual breakfast hour and before the lunch crowd would hit. There wasn't any member of the Tucker family that she could see, only a few customers occupying tables and Mandy, the young waitress, moving about the floor.

Harper slipped inside, found a seat at the table in the corner, and contemplated her choices. It had to be French toast or the cheese and bacon omelet. But coffee, for certain. Nothing fancy, just a big, thick mug of the stuff that she could doctor with real cream, a taste she'd developed during late night cram sessions in college.

Mandy arrived and Harper ordered her beverage and was vacillating between her food choices when Hildie Fontana sailed by, her caftan fluttering, and said, "French toast for the librarian, Mandy. Make sure that the maple syrup served with it is heated."

Harper nodded at the waitress as the older woman took a seat at the next table.

"Um, thanks for the recommendation," Harper ventured when Mandy headed for the kitchen. Then she pulled her e-reader out of her purse.

Hildie leaned closer. "Don't bother, girl," she said. "No need to bury your nose in a book when I'm going to talk your ear off no matter what."

Oh, boy. Harper had heard the owner of the local antique shop was a shameless gossip and had experienced it for herself the first and second times she'd shown up at the library and peppered her with questions about her past, present, and future. But she thought she'd given the woman all the information she was comfortable providing outside of her shoe size and the make and model of her first car.

"That boy," Hildie said now, shaking her head. Her silvery eyebrows moved up and down in a dance all their own. "Good boy. First of those soldier boys of his generation to come back home."

"Um…do you mean Zane?"

"You two have a thing, right? Everybody's saying the librarian is looking at Zane Tucker and he's looking back. I may have heard about some kissing on the sidewalk."

Harper's face burned. "Um…"

"Though he told me you're just friends."

Oh. Deep disappointment cooled her skin. Definitely not going out on the date, Harper thought. Not when he'd just put her in the friend zone. That way led to disaster and heartbreak. She could already write the tragic ending to the story in her head.

"But Zane isn't really the friends-with-women type," Hildie continued.

"What type is he?" Harper asked, before she could stop herself.

"Not to say he isn't friendly to ladies and even with most of them that he's, well, *you know*." Hildie's expressive eyebrows got another workout. "He's just never bothered to make such a declaration about a single eligible woman, as far as I know."

And Hildie, Eagle's Ridge busybody, would know a lot.

But Harper just didn't know what it *meant*.

Hildie continued talking even as Mandy slid coffees in front of both of them and a small steaming pitcher of maple syrup in front of Harper. "In any case, I'm glad he got back safely and was able to work himself through his injuries."

"Injuries?" Mandy now put a fragrant plate of waffles in front of Harper, but even that couldn't distract her from what the older lady had just said. She remembered Zane telling her his shoulder had been hurt, but there'd been no detail beyond him not wanting her to be sad about it.

"They thought he might not move his shoulder or arm again. And he'd lost enough weight that you could see in him that skinny little boy he'd once been."

Harper put her hand over her mouth.

"But he worked at it. Not once did he give into the pain it must have caused him to rehabilitate that shoulder every day on the river and every night at the local gym."

"He looks...well now." Fit. Ripped. Strong. Muscled in a way that made her feminine core melt.

"He is." Hildie nodded, then nodded again to Mandy when she placed before her a plate holding a toasted English muffin and a packet of grape jelly. "He's safely home, with a business he built and with a brother back who has helped him build it into something more. Now he just needs the right woman to make his life complete."

Harper didn't let that last sentence stick. Being Zane's right woman to make his life complete didn't concern her. Tonight did. Because the fact was you couldn't break a date with a once seriously injured Army veteran—no matter how strong he might seem now. Instead you needed to be the prettiest you could be when you sat across the table from him.

Right?

Harper thought about her hair that hadn't been

with a stylist since her move to Eagle's Ridge and her closet that didn't have one date-worthy outfit in it.

An outfit worthy of Zane, anyway.

Or worthy of Stella, either. Because tonight she definitely needed to bring out that more confident, colorful alter-ego.

"Hildie," Harper said, her gaze trained on her plate as she sank her knife into the squishy goodness of the waffle. "Which is the best hair salon in town? And is there a women's clothing boutique you'd recommend?"

"A salon?" A new voice piped up and Harper looked over to see that Jane McAllen was threading through the tables, presumably on her way to the counter. Now she switched directions and came to stand by Harper's table. "And you're looking for a local boutique?"

"I could use some new clothes," Harper confessed, then her hand went to the ends of her hair. "And this stuff grows fast but I haven't found anyone yet to take care of it."

Jane rubbed her hands together. "I'm not the clotheshorse I used to be, but if you want company, I'm your girl. I still love fashion. Not to mention, I do know a great local salon."

"Sure, company would be great." Harper smiled at the other woman who still appeared so *together*, even in dark jeans and a simple shirt. Her shiny hair framed a face that wasn't heavily made up, but had just enough enhancement to polish her appearance. "And maybe you could help me pick out some new mascara and lip color?"

Jane's smile only brightened. "Oh, boy, could I! And your hair's so pretty, I can't wait to see what the stylists at Rosalie's will do with it."

"Do you think they could fit me in today?" Harper asked. "I have a sort of, um, thing tonight."

"Let me see," Jane said, slipping her phone from her back pocket.

Hildie lifted her mug. "Jane will steer you right."

At that moment Brenda bustled up with a pot of coffee and proceeded to top off Harper's mug. As she poured, Jane looked up from her phone. "Hair appointment all set, Harper. Let the makeover begin!"

"Makeover?" Brenda said, turning to Hildie to give her more coffee.

"Yep." Jane stood back on one foot and studied Harper's face. "I think they should take off at least three inches. And get some movement at the ends with layering."

Brenda glanced over. "You're cutting your hair, Harper?"

"I never meant it to get to this length."

"Oh." Brenda's free hand went to the long braid hanging over her shoulder. "I'm not sure I ever meant mine to get this long either. It's just…how I've always worn it."

Jane turned to the older woman, speculation in her gaze. "Brenda…" She drew out the name and the way she did it made it sound like she was dangling a carrot—or maybe a hot fudge sundae. "Would you like to be in on the makeover too?"

"I…um…"

Jane bounced on her heels. "That sounds like a yes!"

So it happened.

Shopping for clothes. Shopping for make-up. Hair appointments, followed by Jane doing both

Harper and Brenda's make-up for them before leaving the salon. Then they all returned for a celebratory round of hot tea at the diner.

Mandy served steaming cups to all three of them and Jane took in the results of her efforts with a more-than-pleased smile on her face.

"Brenda," she said. "You're a beauty."

"Oh. Well." The older woman flushed and her hand flew to her new hairstyle. "I admit I do like it."

The braid was gone. In its place were long layers around her face, and the rest reached no farther than her chin. The stylist had shown Brenda how to use a roller brush to get the volume necessary and the result was chic, but natural-looking. Jane's make-up suggestions were a tinted moisturizer, a delicate line of eyeliner on the edge of her top lashes, taupe shadow on her eyelids and a hint of blush. For her lips, she'd suggested a soft stick that was a bare shade brighter than Brenda's own lips.

Still, she looked younger and fresher and ready to catch any man's attention, especially in a new pair of dark jeans and a pale blue sweater that was slouchy until it hit her hips, where it gathered tightly, accentuating her nice figure. Delicate earrings of gold chain and blue stones hung from her lobes and could be glimpsed through those shining layers of her hair.

"You look wonderful," Harper said.

"As do you."

She couldn't disagree. Though there wasn't a mirror at hand, she absolutely loved what the magician at the salon had done to her hair. The length of it now just brushed her shoulders, and was side-parted. Layers were added around her face and she'd been sold on a product that somehow brought out the wave in her hair. Not as noticeable were the few highlights that made her honey color just a tad more sunny here and there.

Like Brenda, she'd turned herself over to Jane for a make-up lesson and the results boosted her confidence. Her eyes now stood out, their gray framed with dark mascara. Though she wasn't made up for night at the moment, her new friend had shown her how to achieve a more dramatic look that she'd attempt achieving before her date with Zane. Bags from the boutique were gathered around her legs, and inside one of them was the short, pink, white, and black floral skirt that they'd found. It had tiny knife pleats and a black satin ribbon at the waist. She planned on wearing it with a simple black V-neck top that Jane had pulled from the racks and her own black, sling-back pumps.

That outfit was for later. Now, she wore a new pair of dark jeans and paired them with a thin, pretty sweater in pale yellow, that had a triangle-shaped inset of the same color chiffon at the back and tiny covered buttons marching up the middle of it.

"Are you sure you have everything you need for tonight?" Jane asked.

Harper had shared with them both about her plans for the evening and that Zane was taking her to a restaurant some thirty miles away.

"It's a nice place," Brenda said. "The nicest in the area until Bailey opens Blue Moon."

"I think I'm ready," Harper said, pulling in a long breath and letting it out. New hair, new face, new clothes, all of them sure to bring out the Stella in her.

Mischief in her eyes, Jane leaned across the table and lowered her voice. "I wish I could be there to see

Zane's face when he picks you up."

Right then, the door to the kitchen swung open. Sam Tucker strolled out, and Harper was struck by his resemblance to his sons. It was there in the strong build, the confident manner, the handsome features. He wore faded jeans in a way that men half his age would envy, and a pullover sweater, sleeves pushed up to expose his muscle-roped forearms. His mind seemed somewhere else, because he stared straight ahead with a puckered brow, his focus on the diner's entrance as he made for it.

Some new palpable sensation in the air caused Harper to glance in Brenda's direction. *Her* focus was completely on the man, her eyes drinking him in, her body frozen, the teacup halfway to her mouth.

Oh, Harper thought, on a sudden, sympathetic pain. It looked as if Brenda had it bad for her boss and old friend. For confirmation, she shifted her gaze to Jane and they looked at each other, exchanging silent messages.

Gone for him?

Yes. Totally.

He'd nearly passed their table, still without acknowledging the three women or even seeming to be aware of their presence, when Jane spoke up. "Hey, Sam. How's it going?"

His feet stuttered to a stop. He blinked, seeming to come out of his reverie as he peered at the young woman.

"Oh, hello Jane." He ran a hand through his thick hair, obviously still preoccupied. His glance didn't wander to Harper or on to Brenda either.

"Bad day?" Jane chirped. "You're frowning."

"Brenda's going to be late for her shift. I expect

she's lost track of time with another of her dates." He mostly spit out the last word and his expression turned thunderous.

"Are you sure about that?" Jane asked, her tone filled with sugary sweetness and an amusement that Harper detected but Sam apparently didn't.

"She's not answering her phone," he growled.

"Oops," the woman in question said now, reaching into the purse hanging off her chair. "I turned it off at the salon."

At Brenda's words, Sam's head jerked in her direction and his gaze hopscotched over Harper to stare at the diner's manager. His body twitched, his eyes widened.

"This is interesting," Jane whispered, low enough for Harper's ears only.

Several moments of silence passed.

Then Brenda jumped in, her voice a half-octave higher than usual. "But see, I'm here, and not late. So no worries."

Sam's expression morphed from surprise to anger as he continued to take in her face and figure. "What the hell did you do to yourself?" he demanded.

"W-What?" Brenda said.

Sam made a rough gesture in her direction. "*Who* the hell did you do that for?"

Uh-oh. Harper exchanged alarmed looks with Jane.

Brenda's spine snapped straight. "For myself, of course."

"Right," Sam said, the word edged with sarcasm.

The diner manager's eyes narrowed. "Why do *you* think I did it?"

"To get attention," he said instantly.

Brenda jumped to her feet. Her boots snapped against the floor as she moved to stand toe-to-toe with Sam. "Whose attention would that be?"

"The only attention you should care about is mine," he said, staring her down.

Harper and Jane gave each other big eyes as tension crackled in the room.

Brenda's chin jutted up. "And why is that?"

"Because *I* was the one," Sam continued, "who gave you that kiss that I know, I *know* knocked you straight out of your shoes."

Brenda's hands slammed to her hips. "But then you never gave me another one. And you act as if nothing has changed between us. So—"

"So I'm done fighting it," Sam said, his voice rough. "I don't know why the hell I've been fighting it except I'm middle-aged and set in my ways and I don't much like putting my heart out there to be stomped all over by another woman."

On an instant, Brenda's expression turned soft. "Sam." She put her hand on his chest. "I would never do anything to hurt you."

"Good." He placed his hand over hers. "You're coming over once the diner's closed. I'm making dinner. Then you're spending the night."

It was Brenda's turn to twitch. Her free hand went to her new hair. Next she tugged on the hem of her sweater. "Um, think about Max. Your dad is living with you."

Sam's head dropped back, then it righted and he said, "Christ. I'm a middle-aged man, with a father living in the apartment over my garage, and a woman I want to have in my bed." He paused, then his expression set.

"So that's going to happen," the man said, tone decisive. "Dad'll deal."

"You can come to my place," Brenda offered.

"My kitchen, my bed," Sam said, clearly firm on that. "Okay?"

Brenda swallowed, looking like there were some of Gambler's dreaded frogs jumping around in her stomach. "Okay, Sam," she whispered.

"Then see you after close," he said, and started for the door again. When he reached it, Brenda called his name.

"Yeah?" he answered, looking over his shoulder.

She crossed her arms over her chest. "I knocked you straight out of your shoes too."

His sudden grin made him look as young as his sons. "Damn right," he answered, then strode out the exit.

Hours later, Harper was still smiling over what she'd witnessed. But those Gambler frogs had taken up residence in her middle as well, and she put her palm over it as she studied herself in the full-length mirror.

Black pumps.

Knife-pleated, floral print skirt. She tugged on the hem because it was shorter than she remembered.

Short sleeved, V-neck top, also black, also different than she remembered. Clingier.

Jet drops hung from her ears and there was a matching choker around her neck and a delicate bracelet in the same design circling her left wrist.

Too matchy-matchy?

But before she could have time to change anything, her doorbell rang. She gave one last look in the mirror, this time checking her face. The more dramatic eye look she'd learned from Jane had taken a long while to replicate, but she'd done a fair job of it, she thought. Turning from her reflection, she pressed her lips together to make sure her color was evenly distributed as she walked to the front of her condo.

On a deep breath, she pulled open the door.

The frogs in her stomach instantly quieted. Everything inside of her went silent and still as she took in Zane Tucker, wearing dark slacks, dark shoes, a dark gray dress shirt with pinstripes the exact shade of his eyes. Stunning.

She'd never seen a man so beautiful, let alone gone out on a date with one.

Suddenly, her nerves reignited and she regretted not having made a call, or even texted to tell him she was unable to make it tonight.

And then she didn't regret that at all, because as her gaze moved up to his face, she saw that same thunderstruck expression that had been on his father's that afternoon when he'd seen Brenda.

A little of her Stella confidence came back. She placed a hand on her hip. "Well?" she asked.

His brows lowered, his expression turned intense, and she could see the heat that entered his eyes as he continued to take her in. "I'm screwed," he said bluntly.

"Um. Why?"

"I promised myself I'd be a gentleman tonight. But you…in that…" With his hand, he gestured at her body. "Serious jeopardy, sweetheart."

A hot little shiver worked its way down her spine. "You need only be yourself, Zane," she said, and heard the prim note to her voice.

It made him smile. "Then you won't mind when I

rip the head off of any other man who looks at you."

Oh, my. Harper bit back her answering smile.
Though she didn't want him to rip off anybody's
head, of course, it was hard not to feel just the
slightest bit flattered by the unsubtle declaration.

She thought it was going to be a very great date.

Zane worried it was going to be a disaster of a
date. He'd pep-talked to his reflection in the rearview
mirror all the way to her condo—admonishing himself
to be on his best behavior, promising himself he was
going to show the nice woman a nice time, and then
she'd gone and answered her door.

Wearing an outfit that molded her pert breasts
and revealed a long length of bare legs.

She had on those damn black high heels that were
permanently etched into his memory.

And there was something different about her
hair—shorter, maybe? He couldn't pinpoint what,
exactly, but it just seemed to draw attention to the
beauty of her big gray eyes and the puffy temptation
of her delectable mouth.

How the hell was he going to make it to their
table without the whole of the restaurant noticing the
hard-on in his pants?

Pulling into a spot at the rear of the parking lot,
he turned off his truck, then placed his hands back on
the steering wheel, at ten and two, and breathed
deeply, seeking control.

Of course doing so brought her perfume into his
lungs and he recalled the scent of her on his hands
after taking her to bed the other night. Swallowing a
low groan, he squeezed the steering wheel.

"Um, Zane?" she asked, her voice tentative.

"Yeah?" He addressed the windshield, not daring to look at her face again, those eyes, those lips.

"Are we getting out anytime soon?"

"As soon as my dick forgets how damn beautiful you look."

After a startled silence, she laughed, and he had to swallow another groan. Great. She'd think him a real gentleman now.

That thought threw cold water on him, and after another minute he popped open his door and then came around to meet her. She had trouble getting off the high seat in her short dress and he focused on a spot four inches to the right of her shoulder as he put his hands to her waist and helped her down.

He kept his attention away from any dangerous parts of her as they made their way into the restaurant and then were led to their seats. Settled at the corner table he'd reserved, he managed to relax a little. They ordered drinks and appetizers and they both agreed on steaks and a bottle of red with their meal.

With a gin and tonic in front of her and a beer in front of him, he leaned back and felt like, yeah, he could do this.

Harper glanced around at the tables. Each was draped in white linen, with glassware and dinnerware illuminated by the low glow of votive candles. In one corner of the room, logs burned in a massive rock fireplace. The fancy place settings and elegant atmosphere should make him feel as out of place as that bull in a china shop, but with Harper sitting across from him he didn't feel nearly as jumpy as he'd thought he might.

"Is this a favorite place of yours?" she asked.

"I've never brought anyone here before," he said.

"We came once as a family to celebrate Dad's birthday."

"Oh." She looked down at her lap. "It's very nice."

Exactly why he'd thought of it, that and he figured the classy atmosphere might rub off on him—polishing away a few of his roughest edges.

"I was out with Jane today...shopping and such," Harper volunteered, then sipped at her G & T.

"You had fun?"

She nodded. "I did. And I heard about her recent adventures...including her close call."

Zane grimaced. It *had* been close, and his twin had nearly lost his mind when Jane's kayak had capsized in the river and she'd nearly drowned. A fear matching Adam's had pooled in the pit of Zane's gut, and he'd been as spitless as his brother until she'd coughed up the water she'd swallowed and started breathing again.

"Jane was lucky a Coast Guard-trained rescue swimmer was on hand," he said. "That's what Adam used to do before he came back to Eagle's Ridge."

"It seems lucky that you were on hand that day too. You detained the person who tried to kill her?"

He waved that away. "Right place, right time."

"Right training?" she asked. "I think you said you were in the Army?"

"I was. But that had nothing to do with—"

"Brenda told me you were an Army Cavalry Scout."

He smiled, trying to make light of it. "Blame all those Zane Grey novels." Which was more than half the truth.

Harper sipped at her drink again. "She said that

the Cavalry Scouts are the eyes and ears of the
Army."

"That's the broad description." He didn't want to
discuss his time in the military further than that. More
details would only put a blemish on their evening.
Though he wasn't ashamed of his service—far, far
from it—those ten years had been filled with mud,
sand, blood, and bile. Nothing that he wanted her to
connect with him. Not tonight.

"I read up on what all that means," she said.

"Of course you did," Zane muttered. So much for
feigning some kind of veneer of sophistication. If she
did any research, she'd know it was a job that often
required brute strength as much as dogged focus.

Her gray eyes seemed to delve inside his skin and
bones, finding soft, hidden places he would swear he
didn't have. "You're quite the man, Zane Tucker," she
finally said.

Before he could process how that quiet
proclamation affected him, food started arriving and
the topic was left behind. Whew.

Zane had planned some innocuous date patter
during his shower and now he drummed it up, trying
to be smooth despite his inexperience with this kind of
date. His usual evenings out with women involved
playing some pool and drinking beer before drinking
more beer and playing some, well, *pool*. But he and
Harper managed well enough, helped along by the
excellent steaks served with fluffy baked potatoes and
an asparagus gratin.

"I'm going to have to diet after this meal," Harper
said on a sigh, as she set down her knife and fork.
"Carrot and celery sticks are in my immediate future."

"Don't you dare do one thing to compromise that

beautiful ass of yours," Zane instantly said, then just as instantly wanted to punch himself for sounding so…uncivilized. *Beautiful ass*. It was true, of course, but he could have put it more politely.

She was staring at him, round-eyed.

"It's that little skirt," he muttered. "Okay? It's making me kind of crazy."

"Oh." A smile flirted with the corners of her mouth.

It eased some of his tension. Maybe the librarian hadn't taken offense.

He figured he was right about that after another few minutes when she excused herself for the ladies' room. Because as she walked away, she took a quick glance over her shoulder, saw he was watching, and added a decided swing to her hips.

Zane didn't even try to fight off his grin.

It died when a pair of arms wrapped around his neck from behind. "Hey, handsome."

He turned his head to meet the velvet brown gaze of Marla Hopper. They'd gone out a few times before she'd had to temporarily move to Oregon to care for her mother after back surgery. "How are you?" he asked the tall, buxom brunette. "How's your mom?"

"I'm good. In the area again now that my mother can take care of herself."

"Great news," he said, and as she loosened her hold, he shifted his chair to converse more easily.

Marla took it as an invitation to slip into his lap.

Shit. "Uh…" He had no idea where to put his hands and wondered how to make clear he was on a date.

Before an answer presented itself, Harper returned to their table. Taking in the scene, her eyebrows rose toward her hairline.

"Uh…" he said again, and got to his feet at the same moment that Marla jumped to hers.

"I'm sorry," she said, looking at the librarian. "I didn't realize…"

"No problem." In a practiced, polite move, Harper held out her hand and introduced herself.

Marla reciprocated, then added, "I've been out of the area for a couple of months. With my mom as she recuperated from surgery."

"You probably haven't heard then," Harper said kindly. "Zane and I…well, we're an item."

He stared at her. That gossip *was* all over Eagle's Ridge and its environs, of course, but to hear her claim it…damn, but it made a contented warmth settle in his chest. Dumbfounded by the feeling, he stood silently watching as the two women continued to chat.

Two such different women. Marla was a female version of himself, a lively person who liked to drink beer, shoot pool, and was the best dart player in two counties.

Harper, on the other hand, had a much quieter presence. But for some reason it only leant an intriguing bit of mystery to her, and challenged him to peel back her layers. He wanted to do things to test that reserve of hers—to make her spontaneously smile, laugh, sigh, and then shatter any and every one of her inhibitions.

"I'll see you around," Marla said now to Zane, brushed her lips against his cheek, then smiled a little. "I'd tell you to call me, but…"

He glanced at Harper. "I'm going to be pretty busy."

As the brunette wandered back to the bar, he

unearthed his best manners and held out Harper's chair for her. She glanced up at him as she lowered into it, smiled, and that warmth bloomed in his chest again.

"Dessert," he said, as he settled into his own seat. "We'll share."

The waitress only brought one fork and he didn't ask for another. Leaning across the table, he fed bites of chocolate molten lava cake to Harper, fascinated by the soft look on her face and the tidy way she patted her napkin to her lips.

Still, she missed a spot, and he didn't hesitate to touch his forefinger to the corner of her mouth, then dragged it slowly across her bottom lip. Her breath caught, and he saw her eyes dilate.

Zane's own muscles tightened and his free hand shot up to flag the waitress. "I think I need to get you home," he said, his voice gruff.

Before he went full caveman on her and dragged her across the table linens and fancy dishes to get a taste of the librarian.

Once outside, he held her hand while they crossed the parking lot toward his truck. The cool air did nothing to lessen the heat of his blood and the thrum of anticipation in his body. "It was a lovely meal," Harper said, her small fingers curled trustingly in his. "Thank you."

"You're welcome." A lovely meal, a lovely woman, a lovely date. He'd managed not to blow it, despite a few lapses here and there. Maybe he had a domesticated side after all.

Then a muffled shout from the opposite corner of the parking lot caught his attention. He glanced that way and saw three men scuffling with one another.

It took a second moment to recognize that one of the scufflers was Denver, the ranch hand whose cowboy boots now sat in Zane's closet. He recognized the other pair as river guides for the North Snake Adventures outfit. *Hell.*

"Stay here," he told Harper, and took off at a run toward the fracas. Once closer to the trio, he deduced that Denver had wrested car keys away from the obviously drunken North Snake guys—and they strenuously objected to the precaution. Both seemed to believe that either one of them was capable of driving home.

Even sober, Zane didn't think much of the guides, but overserved they were beyond stupid and bordering on nasty. Into their eff-bomb laden diatribe, Zane boomed a question.

"Got a problem, Denver?"

The younger man looked grateful as he came to stand by his side. "You know these guys, Zane? Tonight they shouldn't be driving."

"I know them." And why the hell they'd been at this nice dinner house and how the hell they'd managed to hide from the bartender they were drunk as skunks, he couldn't say. "Boys, why don't we call you a car service? Safer for everyone."

"Safer my ass," one slurred. "Now gimme my keys."

Zane took them from Denver and shoved them deep in his pocket. "Not a good idea. What I think—"

A fist came up and rammed into Denver's face. He buckled, his hands going to his nose.

Shit. Zane moved in front of him. "Now—"

The boxer took another swing. Zane couldn't duck, that would expose Denver again, so he caught the guy's wrist. "Hey—"

Then pain exploded in his face as the second guy's fist made contact with it.

Now it was he who dropped an eff bomb as the two river guides went nuts, letting fly with the insults and with their arms. Denver stepped from behind Zane and grunted as he took another blow to the face.

"Damn it, get back," Zane said to his smaller friend, as he shoved Drunk One away. The guy stumbled back, tripping over his own feet to fall on his ass. Drunk Two took offense on his buddy's behalf, and with a Viking cry, launched himself at Zane. His forehead thumped into Zane's nose, causing sparks to fly in his vision. But he managed to wrap the skinny dude in a bear hug before getting head-butted a second time.

"Shit!" Zane lifted the fighter off his feet, and then flung him away. The man stumbled around, weaving like the drunk he was, and hadn't regained his balance when a sheriff's cruiser pulled up.

The situation was quickly managed—river guides in the back of the cruiser, statements given by Denver and Zane—and then the manager of the restaurant came running out with paper napkins to staunch the blood dripping from Denver's nose.

And from Zane's.

Shit. Hell. Damn. He looked at Harper hovering nearby, the lights from the sheriff's car illuminating her wide eyes and alarmed expression. Then he glanced down at his heavily stained shirt and the wad of bloody tissues in his hand.

The poor woman looked freaked out.

Over a parking lot brawl, that was not, by any means, Zane's first.

He sighed, the earlier warmth in his chest displaced by a sharp pain that ran parallel to the aching throb coming from his face.

He was no gentleman. Not any kind of man for the pretty lady librarian.

Chapter 8

Harper let three days pass. Three days without hearing from Zane or seeing him. The morning after their dinner, she'd sent him a quick text thanking him again for the meal and asking how he fared after the clash in the parking lot. He'd responded with "You're welcome" and "I'm good" but nothing more.

She didn't know what was on his mind. After the sheriff said they could leave, Zane had driven her home and walked her to her door in silence. When she'd offered a bag of peas from her freezer, he'd claimed to have one at home and had taken off after a single quick squeeze of her shoulder.

Then, she'd figured he wanted to get out of his bloody clothes.

Now, she wondered if he'd wanted to get away from her.

But the date had been great up until those moments in the parking lot. Had she been wrong about that?

Tired of debating the subject with herself, Harper took a chance and walked to No Man's Land during her morning break. There, she counted luck on her side because she found Jane at the counter, sipping hot tea, with Brenda on the other side, her own mug in hand. Only two other patrons were in the diner, each at their own corner and engrossed in their food and phones.

"I was just going to head to the library and check out a book," Jane said as Harper slid onto the stool beside hers.

"Which book are you interested in?" Harper asked.

"The Book of What Happened Monday Night." The other young woman sent a sly smile toward the diner manager. "Our friend here is keeping the cover on hers stubbornly closed. I only asked for a summary and she won't even provide that."

Brenda's eyes slid in the direction of the kitchen. "Jane! I can't let my boss hear me gossiping—"

"Especially about him," Jane said, with another cheeky smile. "I get it. That's why Harper must satisfy my prurient interest."

"I have nothing salacious to report," Harper admitted.

Jane's eyes widened. "But...but...your hair, your outfit. All fabulous. I was sure his tongue would unroll to his toes."

"It kind of did," Harper said, feeling a smile grow as she remembered the wowed expression on Zane's face. "And he said he didn't want other men to look at me." At the comment, her ego had soared, and the defection of Geoffrey had instantly receded a quarter-mile farther in her personal rearview mirror.

Jane clapped. "After that…"

"Well, after we finished our entrées, I went to the restroom and when I came out another woman was sitting on his lap."

"What hussy was this?" Brenda demanded.

"Her name was Marla and she was actually nice. I think she was embarrassed by the situation. I know Zane was. Then I made it clear to her that he was taken." She paused. "By me."

Jane's smile dazzled. "You rock."

"I kind of did." Harper returned the grin. "I didn't know I was going to say it, but I did, and then she went away and then Zane and I shared a dessert, and then…" A shiver worked its way down her spine as she recalled his finger running along her bottom lip and the heat in his eyes as he called for the check.

"Then?" Brenda prompted.

"Then in the parking lot we ran into some drunk guys and Zane tried to help his friend. Punches were thrown, blood was shed, and a sheriff's deputy arrived." She shrugged. "I guess the altercation kind of killed the mood."

Which she'd accepted at the time, but now couldn't they pick up where they'd left off?

"Outside of a brief exchange of text messages, he hasn't contacted me since," she told the other women, then sighed. "I really don't know what to think or do now."

"Sometimes we Tuckers can be a little slow on the uptake," a new voice said.

Harper looked over to see Sam framed by the pass-through.

Brenda's lips twitched. "You can say that again."

He grinned at her. "Sometimes we Tuckers can be

a little slow on the uptake." He let a beat pass. "Then we more than make up for it, don't we, Bren?"

The older woman blushed. "Sam," she scolded. "Enough of that."

Harper recalled Monday afternoon and the way Zane's father had taken charge of the stalled situation with the diner manager. Once he'd declared he was done fighting against their connection, Brenda's resistance had melted. Tilting her head, Harper considered a similar action. Evidence suggested Zane had been pleased when she'd been direct with Marla at the restaurant.

Maybe Harper needed to be direct with the man himself now.

Though she'd lost her nerve that day in the library a while back and shied away from asking him out, couldn't she show some backbone now and ask him for, well, more?

She looked to Jane. "Do you know anything about this afternoon's schedule at A To Z?"

"I know that I can conspire with Adam to make Zane free, even if he isn't," the other woman said promptly.

"Do it." Harper jumped off her stool. "I plan to show up there at four o'clock."

At 3:59, she stood in front of A To Z Watersports, which was housed in what must have once been a big family residence. Though the sky was overcast, the balmy temperature was probably the reason only a screen door covered the front entrance, and she looked curiously at the misshapen bulge in the bottom half of the wire mesh. Then, shrugging, she let herself inside, obeying the "Come On In" sign hanging from the door's handle.

Indoors, music played, something with a bluegrass flavor. It smelled like old wood and dark coffee, and she breathed in the comforting mingled scents. To her right was a room that probably had once been a parlor, but now looked like a reception area. Zane sat on the edge of the desk there, one hand on the keyboard of a laptop, his attention split between that device and his cell phone.

He hadn't heard her come in, so she took a moment to catalog his features.

A little soundless sigh escaped her lips. He was so, so…man. From the dark unruly hair on the top of his head to the black running shoes on his feet. He wore workout pants and a skin-tight, short-sleeved shirt and it looked like he hadn't shaved since their Monday night date.

Even his whiskers were manly, bristles dark and uncompromising, and they served to accentuate the soft looking curves of his lips.

His kiss would taste hot and sweet, but be edged by that rough, exciting stubble.

Harper's inner thighs clenched. She wanted more of him all right.

Suddenly, his head shot up. "Harper." His expression registered surprise followed swiftly by wariness.

She remained still under his regard, glad she'd donned bright white running tights splashed with purple and turquoise and a purple top that fit snug to her hips. Both were new. Both didn't hide a single curve.

Don't you dare do one thing to compromise that beautiful ass of yours.

The memory gave her the confidence to move

forward, with not quite a swagger, and maybe not quite a saunter, but with real purpose. "Hello, Zane."

He eyed her approach. "Um…"

"I'm here," she said.

"I see that," he replied, definitely wary.

"Because you owe me."

His mouth turned down in a grimace. "You're right. Before now I should have called or come by with an apology."

It was her turn for surprise. "An apology for what?"

"Monday night, of course. You certainly didn't say yes to going out with me expecting to end the evening in violence and bloodshed."

She blinked. "I had a great time Monday night…well, I didn't like seeing you getting hit in the face, but before that I enjoyed myself immensely. And to be honest…"

"Yes?"

"I thought the fight was a little exciting," she confessed. "I knew you had things under control."

He stared at her.

She half-shrugged.

With a shake of his head, he straightened from his seat on the edge of his desk and put both feet on the scarred hardwood floor. "Okay, then."

There was dismissal in his voice. He thought he was going to get rid of her now? Um, no.

She put her hand on her hip. "What you owe me is a training run, Zane. I'm dressed for it. You're dressed for it. Let's go."

"Right now? But I—"

"Have no excuse. Jane told me Adam is covering your afternoon kayak class."

His brows drew together. "My brother said he wanted to get out on the water to clear his head."

"Which frees *you*," she pointed at him, "to take *me*," her thumb hit her chest, "out for some training."

When he didn't immediately refuse, she sidled closer and put her hand on his arm. His head bent to stare at it, and she felt his muscles harden under her touch.

"Please?"

He growled something under his breath, and then he cleared his throat. "You're still determined to compete in the event?"

"Of course," she said. "Even if I have to crawl across the finish line. But I'd prefer to do it upright, so…"

"All right, all right," he said begrudgingly, then moved away from her hand. "Let me get us each a bottle of water."

This time, Zane opted to leave Gambler behind and the dog barely looked up from his snooze on a massive pet bed in the old kitchen that appeared to be used as a breakroom for the business. Then they slipped out the back door, stretching for a few minutes before taking off at an easy pace on a path leading into the surrounding forest.

The pace was easy enough to make conversation possible, but twenty minutes in, she could tell that conversation was something Zane planned to avoid.

Too bad, Harper thought.

"That steak was really amazing the other night. Thanks again."

He grunted.

She mentally rolled her eyes.

"I enjoyed getting dressed up for you." Hah, try

grunting in response to that!

His eyes slid her way. "I'm not going to deny you looked amazing," he said, his voice gruff. "Fine. You looked damned hot."

"Nobody's arguing with you." *But yourself,* she thought. *You're working so hard to pretend this thing between us doesn't exist.*

Then, knowing it would take her straight off Santa's good girl list, she pretended to slip on the damp earth. Zane's hand immediately shot out and banded her bicep, hauling her close so that the sides of their bodies kissed.

His skin's heat transferred to her. "Are you okay?" he asked, looking down at her.

She let herself get lost in his eyes, their color that arresting combination of blue and green. Thinking again of Sam's directness, she gathered her courage. "I want more, Zane. More with you. More of you."

He froze, though his fingers tightened on her arm. "Not a good idea, Harper."

"The town already—"

"The town might be talking about us, but we don't have to make that talk come true."

Frustration drew her brows together. Why was he fighting so hard? She could see his chest rising and falling roughly, and it had nothing to do with the short jog they'd just taken. It was her proximity, that chemistry between them that made the air hum and made her feel so…exciting and womanly.

Sexy.

And wanting. Wanting him.

His fingers on her loosened one by one, seemingly reluctant as the rest of him.

Harper barely suppressed stamping her foot.

Really, must he be so damn stubborn?

"What is it about me?" she demanded. "Why are you so willing to walk away from something I know you feel as much as me?"

He rubbed his hand over the bottom half of his face and she could almost feel the scratch of his whiskers against her own palm. "It's just that…"

But she knew exactly what it was, she decided, thinking back to the things he'd said to her in the past couple of weeks. "It's because you think we're so different, isn't it?" She glared up at him. "Because you see me as a city girl, and as a society girl, someone who is too soft or too fussy for you and your world."

"That's not it." A glimmer of a smile touched his lips. "I like your soft and I like your fussy."

Her hands came to her hips and her glare didn't abate. "Then I know exactly what it is. Like every damn arrogant man in the world, you are quaking in your shoes thinking I'm going to fall in love with you. That then I'm going to want to marry you."

He stared down at her, his expression bemused.

When he didn't break the silence, she continued on. "But see, I'm not looking to fall in love. And maybe I want to get married someday, but it will be to someone who actually wants that too, or otherwise it's Geoffrey all over again."

She poked the big man in the center of his hard chest with a fingertip. "All I'm asking for, Zane Tucker, is more of you. More of you and me, with no expectations attached. It can be as casual as you want."

His silence continued.

"Well?" She lifted her arms to her sides. "What

do you have to say to that?"

In answer, he grabbed her by the shoulders, yanked her close, and then up to her toes.

Next he kissed her.

It started to rain, the drops cold against her skin, but it didn't lessen the heat pulsing beneath her flesh. His tongue drove inside her mouth and as her body trembled, her last thought before passion completely stole her away was that she hoped she'd told him the truth, the whole truth, and nothing but the truth.

Harper bustled about her office in the library as closing time approached. A swift glance out the half-glass wall indicated that no patrons lingered near the exit or in the study rooms, but after she tidied her desk she'd make a last walkthrough before locking the doors.

Shoving pencils into the mug beside her blotter, she noted the slight pink sunburn on the back of her hand. She smiled at the sight, recalling Zane giving her what he called a "taste of the river." Though his schedule was crazy-busy as the tourist season progressed, he'd managed to free a few hours one recent afternoon to take her on an easy raft ride, a short spin in the kayak, and then helped her don a wetsuit to try out a paddle board. Of course she'd ended up drenched, but exhilarated too.

Nearly a week had passed since she'd ambushed him at A To Z, and despite his work obligations they'd managed that watery afternoon, a late dinner before the diner closed, and drinks and cheese fries at Baldie's. There'd been no more overt resistance from him—as a matter of fact, their outings had all been his idea—but what there also hadn't been was sex.

Aware that it was she who had proclaimed their relationship could be as casual as he wanted, she'd been obligated to follow his lead on intimacy. Kisses. Hugs. Holding hands.

Knowing also that he worked long hours doing very physical labor, she'd told herself to be content and not demand any more from him. If her doubts and insecurities voiced that he might be hesitating to take her to bed again as a way to keep some distance between them—or because their earlier experience between the sheets hadn't blown his mind as it had hers—she'd ignored their insidious murmurings and carried on.

Throwing her purse strap over her shoulder, she headed out of her office for a last walkthrough, keys in hand. The place seemed deserted. Then, in one of the reading areas, where two couches formed an L, she found a final patron stretched on the cushions.

Sound asleep.

A Longmire mystery lay open on his chest.

Her breath caught in hers.

A glow seemed to light her insides as she gazed on Zane, his long form in jeans, boots, another waffle-weave Henley. Then, as if even in his dozing state he could sense her presence, his eyes blinked open. Their otherworldly blue-green shocked her all over again and she couldn't look away from them as he swung his legs around and sat up.

His smile was sleepy and sweet and felt like an arrow straight to the middle of her heart. "Hey," he said.

"Hey." She smiled back.

"I came in near closing time to catch you—to see if you wanted to get some dinner together—but you were talking to your assistant in your office and then I sat down with a book, and then…" He shrugged. "Quick trip to Snoozeville."

"Long days for you," she said.

"Dawn hike this morning, followed by a guided kayak run and then rafting in the afternoon. Same thing tomorrow."

Harper held out her hand to him. "Then you need a good home-cooked meal and I know right where you can get one. My place."

She'd walked to the library so he drove her home in his truck. Then she set him up at her condo's kitchen bar with a beer and some cheese and crackers and she threw together a meal of meatloaf, roasted red potatoes, and a green salad with a vinaigrette dressing.

"I can help," he said, as she chopped a cucumber.

"No need." She waved the offer away. Then she glanced over at him. "Do you know how to cook? I guess you must, what with your dad running the diner."

"Yeah, I can flip a burger and make a mean grilled cheese and bacon sandwich—No Man's Land fare. After our mother left for Hollywood, Bailey took over the home kitchen and made meals that would tempt Dad to the table for family dinners."

He tipped back his bottle of beer to take a swallow. "But when I was that sickly kid stuck indoors, I often watched my mom make a pot roast or stuffed pork chops. When I didn't feel like eating, she'd make my favorite—chicken soup from scratch."

Harper paused, her knife hovering over the vegetable. "That sounds…caring."

He studied the label on his bottle for a moment. "Truth to tell, when she was there, at our home in

Eagle's Ridge, she was great. A great mother. When I was sick and couldn't leave the house, she promised me I would get better. She told me I'd have everything I ever wanted and that I would beat the illness."

He cleared his throat. "I believed her."

"And it happened," Harper said softly. "You got better. You live a full life."

"But then opportunity knocked and she got a chance to portray the mother in the family drama *Mother May I*."

"Oh." Everybody knew that popular TV show. It had run for years. "A pretty big opportunity, then."

"Right." His thumb swept through the sweat on his beer, his expression thoughtful. "She chased her dream and caught up with it."

Instead of commenting further, Harper opted for more generic chit chat next, until she could serve up the hot, home-cooked meal that she'd promised. Zane dug in, had seconds, then insisted on doing the dishes. She watched him move about her small kitchen, smiling when his elbow knocked the paper towels off the counter and he bumped his head on the low-hanging fixture.

"I'm sorry," she offered.

"Don't be," he answered, ruefully rubbing at the crown of his head. "This is my life."

One she couldn't help but hope would include her. In a casual way, she hastily reminded herself. Without expectation of anything more than the kisses-only friendship he seemed content with at the moment. But a slow pace wouldn't kill her, she decided, though she hoped for something more intimate eventually.

With the kitchen cleaned up, he seemed in no hurry to go. They took their places on the couch in her living room, the TV tuned to baseball. Though not much of a sports fan, Harper didn't care. She enjoyed his company and even more so when he put his arm around her shoulders and hauled her close. As she lifted her mouth to place a kiss on his jawline, she heard her phone ring in her purse, hanging over a barstool in the other room.

His hand drifted down her back as she stood to retrieve it.

Her mom was on the other end of the call. Harper remained in the kitchen, puzzled and a bit alarmed. "Is everything okay?" she immediately asked. As a general rule, her mother refused to use her phone after six o'clock, reserving the evening hours for uninterrupted time with her husband.

Harper figured it wasn't a bad idea, as her dad had been devoted to her mother for thirty-four years.

"Everything's fine," her mother said, but there was an odd note to her voice. "And you? Are you fine?"

Harper thought of the man in the other room. Oh, she was *so* fine, even if she had to wait for ages to be skin-to-skin with Zane again. He'd been such a patient teacher on the water and such a pleasant companion off of it. No man had ever made her feel so…protected. And heard. And seen. When he smiled at her, it was as if they were the only two in the world.

"I'm terrific, Mom," she said.

"Job going well? You still like Eagle's Ridge?"

"The job is great. I'm liking Eagle's Ridge very much."

"Oh." Her mom sounded disappointed, and

Harper assumed she was still holding on to hope that her younger daughter would return to San Francisco.

That wasn't going to happen. "And Mom..."

"Yes?"

Harper hauled in a breath. "I've met someone."

"A new friend you mean?"

"A man." She lowered her voice, her gaze drifting in the direction of the living room where she could hear the TV still played the game. "I like him. I like him very, very much."

"Oh," her mother said again, this time sounding not just disappointed, but maybe uneasy.

Harper frowned. "Mom? What is it?"

"Nothing, nothing!" Patricia Grace said with a forced gaiety. "But I hear your father calling. You know how he insists I sit beside him during the *PBS News Hour.*"

Before Harper could get to the bottom of her parent's strange behavior, her mom ended the call. "Hmm," she said, as she made for the living room. "Weird."

Zane still occupied her couch. But he'd half-slumped against one round arm and looked to be out cold. One beer wouldn't do that.

Dawn hike this morning, followed by a guided kayak run and then rafting in the afternoon. Same thing tomorrow.

Pure physical exhaustion would do that.

Loathe to wake him, she crossed to the couch and knelt at his feet where she undid the laces of his boots. She eased them off and then drew his legs up onto the couch. His lax expression didn't change. Not a single muscle twitched.

From the back of a nearby chair, she plucked a

folded blanket. Then she tossed it over him and spent some minutes tucking it around his big body. Finally, she stood over the man, gazing on him in sleep.

Just like at the library, a warm glow ignited inside her.

Bending, she brushed his hair off his forehead, but didn't even bother to kiss his cheek. Because gazing upon him at rest made clear there were all kinds of intimacy.

Having him here, where she could watch over him as he recharged, was one of the sweetest.

Chapter 9

Zane finagled a rare Saturday off during the season by bribing one of their new river guides with an entire weekend free at the end of the summer. Still, he stopped in the office in the early morning to make a final check.

Adam sauntered into the kitchen/breakroom, the wind having wreaked havoc with his hair and the early morning chill bringing a ruddy color to his cheeks and forehead. He'd led the dawn hike that was followed by the popular kayak run. Nodding at Zane, he moved directly toward the full pot of coffee.

"I will live," he said, after pouring himself a mug and drinking half of it down.

"Good to know," Zane said, pinning the next day's schedule onto the bulletin board. It was on the computer and he'd sent it to the phones of each and every guide, but it never hurt to have it posted in another place as well.

"I haven't heard details of your plans for today,"

Adam said.

"I'm first escorting Gambler to the library. It's a Kids Reading to Dogs day." Zane felt an absurd burst of pride. "Bella, the little girl who read to him two weeks ago, has especially asked for a repeat." Though her "Uncle Noah" had returned to DC, he'd passed along the child's request to Zane via text.

"I can't believe he sits still for that." Adam gestured toward the long scratches in the molding around the back door. "That's yesterday's work when Holly came through the front tooting on a kazoo. She got it as a promotional gimmick from that new bookstore in town and the sound of it sent him into a frenzy."

"Oh, hell," Zane said. "Put it on—"

"The Terror List. I know. It's been duly updated."

Adam took another swallow of his coffee. "So you're going to spend the day with Harper?"

"I'll see her at the library," he said, not committing to more than that. But God, he wanted to see her, see her alone and when he wasn't dog-tired. Two nights before he'd fallen asleep on her couch and hadn't had a chance to apologize in person. The following morning, it had been his turn to lead the dawn hike so he'd had to leave her house while it was still dark and she was still sleeping.

"C'mon Bro," Adam said. "You have the whole day off. You gotta spend some time with your woman."

His woman. "She's not that."

"Oh, really?"

"Look, I'm taking it slow. Being careful because I don't want to hurt her," Zane said. "You know how clumsy I can be."

"Please." Adam shook his head. "You're nearly as accomplished an athlete as I am."

Zane snorted at that.

Adam's lips twitched, but he carried on. "Seriously. You have never gone out of your way to hurt a woman. I've never heard a woman complain that you did so."

"Harper's a different type than I usually...associate with. I can't explain it."

"So? Tastes change. People change."

Zane grimaced. "I'm starting to hate that word," he mumbled. "Really hate it."

Adam stilled, his eyes narrowing. "What's up with all this?" he demanded. "Why are you so frickin' grumpy?"

"Does a man have to be sunshine and sugar goddamn cubes all the time?"

Adam's stared a moment longer, then his perplexed expression cleared. "You're not getting it from her, are you?"

Sometimes Zane hated the twin mind-reading thing. The back of his neck burned and he looked down at his feet. "I told you," he muttered. "I don't want to hurt her by leading her on, or leading her to believe I'm some kind of forever material. So taking it...slow."

"I've seen you holding her hand," Adam said, now looking incredulous. "Giving her little smooches at the diner."

"Smooches?" Zane lifted a brow.

"Face it, Bro, you've smooched her in public. She obviously liked it. If you haven't taken that any farther, the poor woman's probably wondering if there's something wrong with you. Or worse, if there's something wrong with her. That you don't find her truly desirable."

Oh, shit. There was nothing wrong with Harper, that wasn't why he hadn't hopped into bed with her again. Instead, he'd wanted to show her some respect, and to show some restraint so she'd know he didn't see her as a simple booty call. But instead he'd sent the wrong message?

Talk about clumsy.

Because, damn it, he did find her desirable, oh-so-effing desirable.

Shoving his hand into his pocket for his keys, he headed out of A To Z, desperate to get some time alone with her now. He'd find the words to explain. She needed to know that he wanted her in a powerful way.

He and Gambler were two minutes early for the Kids Reading to Dogs program. But if he thought he might have a moment or two alone with the librarian, he was wrong. Already canines and kids were gathered and she was directing them to seats even as she lugged a stack of books around the back patio.

He hustled up to help her with the load, but some clean-cut, fastidious-looking dad beat him to it. The man didn't notice the scowl Zane sent his way.

Harper didn't seem to notice Zane was even in attendance other than pointing out where Gambler should wait for Bella. He got the dog situated on the same blanket under the same tree as before and waited expectantly for the child's arrival. Gambler seemed anxious too, letting out little whines until he caught sight of the little girl—again dressed in pink and glitter.

This time, she arrived with Wyatt Chandler, who

watched Bella drop down onto the blanket with her book, then strolled over to where Zane was standing off to the side.

"Hey," Wyatt said, bracing against the library's back wall, in the same pose as Zane.

"Hey, back. You're on Bella patrol?"

"Yeah. Her mom's not doing well and Noah's back in DC. He asked if I could help out. Happy to."

But the other man, a former SEAL used to action and adventure, didn't look all that excited to be assigned childcare duties. "I know a guy who runs a team of bike couriers in LA. Swears the survival rush at the end of each day is unbeatable. I've even got an old Schwinn Stingray—I think it was my dad's—you could have for a song."

"Shut up, Zane."

"Or then there's…" His words trailed off as Harper hurried by again. Before, he'd only registered her slightly harried expression and the heavy burden she carried. Now, unencumbered, he saw that she wore dark, tight jeans with high-heeled boots. A cherry-red, short-sleeved sweater hugged her in all the right places and he thought she must have snuck away to reapply her lipstick, because her bow-shaped mouth now matched the color of her top.

His blood began to chug, slow and deliberate, as his gaze drank her in.

The poor woman's probably wondering if there's something wrong with her. If you don't find her truly desirable.

Without thinking, he started for her, determined to clear up any of her misapprehensions. Wyatt's snigger stopped him.

Zane's head turned toward his old friend.

"What?" he demanded.

All of a sudden, the other man was looking infinitely more cheerful.

"*What?*" Zane said again.

"Mighty. Fallen," Wyatt said, sounding both smug and amused.

"I don't know what the hell you're talking about." Zane forced his shoulder blades back to the wall. Patience. He couldn't just accost the woman while she was at work and convince her of his undying lust.

"You've got it bad."

"I still don't know what you're talking about."

"The librarian. You," Wyatt said. "You're in love with her."

Lust, damn it. "Let's talk about something else."

Wyatt's eyes were lit with an unholy glee. "Let's talk about a bet."

Zane glanced over at his friend. There was just something about a bet—making one or taking one—that he couldn't resist. Blame his DNA. Blame his asthmatic childhood that necessitated he learn to amuse himself in myriad ways. "What are you wanting to wager?" he asked slowly.

"I trust you, Zane. You're as honest as the day is long."

"Thanks…I think." There was a trap in there somewhere.

"I'll give you…ten days. If by the end of that time you tell me truly you aren't a goner for the librarian, I'll buy that bike off you. But if you admit to what I know is true, then you have to…well, I'll figure out just the right thing later."

What the hell? It was reckless, since Wyatt wasn't specifying his side of the wager, but that didn't matter. Zane was safe. He jonesed after Harper, in an earthy, physical way, and it didn't go any deeper than that. It would never be any deeper. That wouldn't change in ten days or in ten years.

"You're on." They shook on it.

It might have been a decade, though, before the kids and dogs program came to a conclusion. Sweet Bella thanked both him and Gambler for the experience and then went off with Wyatt, who sent Zane a farewell smirk.

He responded with a subtle middle finger sliding up the side of his face. Then he trailed Harper around the patio as she gathered books, folded blankets, and was completely engrossed in conversations with grateful parents and chatty little kids.

Finally, he figured out that the librarian wasn't going to manage a minute for him during her time at the library. And maybe it wasn't the proper setting to discuss how much he wanted to get her into a bed and how quickly they could find one anyway.

Your place or mine didn't seem an appropriate question for a Saturday in the library stacks at Eagle's Ridge.

So, knowing Gambler only had a short time limit before causing something calamitous, he snagged Harper's elbow. Her big gray eyes lifted to his.

Hell. So pretty.

"Everything okay?" she asked.

"No," he muttered.

Her lashes fluttered. "Um…"

"We need to talk."

"Um…"

"You have a break coming up?"

She swallowed, pink color blossoming on her

cheeks. He must look as horny as he felt. "I'm off for the day at 1:00," she said.

He'd feed her first. They'd need their energy so he could show her exactly how much he wanted her. "Meet me at No Man's Land, yeah?"

Her eyes flared wider. "Yeah."

Halfway to satisfied, he took off for the diner to wait. After he led his dog to his comfortable bed and bowl of water in the storeroom, he spied Ryder at a table, a glass of iced tea and the remains of a burger and fries in front of him. He flung himself into a chair beside the other man, the action rocking the table.

Ryder glanced over and then his brows rose. "What's up? You look like a coiled spring."

"Waiting on a woman."

"Ah," Ryder said, and picked up a fry, dipped it in a puddle of ketchup. "The librarian."

"We're going to get a few simple things straight as soon as she arrives," he said.

"Good luck with that," Ryder replied. "In my experience, getting things straight with a woman isn't ever very simple."

But when Harper arrived not long later, Zane saw it all with sudden, crystal clarity. Enough of this handholding and worrying about moving too fast or moving at all, he decided. Sex would definitely straighten out the tangles and knots that had been plaguing him for days.

Her eyes shifted to him and he rose from his chair.

As their eyes met, he could swear the chemical reaction between the two of them caused the molecules in the room to rub against each other like lovers in heat. The electricity generated by the anticipation of them coming together once more, without any clothes or second thoughts between them, could run all the neon beer signs at Baldie's.

Harper began to slowly move toward him as lust pounded in his bloodstream and his heart knocked against his chest. The diner door behind her opened again. His gaze didn't leave her face, however, until he heard her name in another man's voice.

"Harper?" the stranger said.

She glanced back.

"Harper," the man said again, holding out his arms. "It's me."

Now she half-turned, her expression stunned. "Geoffrey?"

Geoffrey?

"Who the hell is Geoffrey?" Ryder muttered.

"The guy who jilted her," Zane said through clenched teeth as he swiftly made for *his* woman.

Not swiftly enough that he didn't catch Ryder's next muttered comment. "What the hell? When did No Man's Land become a bad-ex magnet?"

"I need to talk to you," Geoffrey said to Harper.

It was then that many things occurred to her all at once. Geoffrey Giffin was shorter than she remembered. His hair thinner. His skin paler.

And dressed in a cashmere sweater, black slacks, and well-polished black loafers, he looked completely out of place among the jeans, tees, and flannels of the other diners in No Man's Land.

"What are you doing here?" she asked. "How did you even know where to find me?"

"The woman at the desk in the library told me she thought you'd gone to the restaurant on the bridge."

She pressed two fingers to the sudden throb in her right temple. "I mean, how did you know to find me in Eagle's Ridge, Washington?" They'd not had another conversation after she'd handed back his ring and that same day she'd blocked his phone number.

"Your mother told me," Geoffrey said.

Maybe her parent's strange call a couple of nights before made more sense. "So Mom contacted you?"

"I contacted her. I was...surprised and disappointed to discover you'd left San Francisco." Her ex's gaze suddenly shifted from her face to someone over her shoulder.

Harper didn't have to turn around to know that someone was Zane, who had come up behind her. She could feel the heat and size of him at her back and she wished Geoffrey away with all her might.

We need to talk, Zane had said in the library. That had sounded so promising!

What wasn't promising, was the stubborn set to Geoffrey's mouth and the words he'd just uttered. *Surprised and disappointed.*

"Really," she said, frowning at him. "I can't imagine why anything I would do would cause you surprise or disappointment. We're no longer connected in any way."

"I made a mistake about that." Geoffrey glanced around at the crowded tables. "Maybe we could go somewhere more private to talk?"

A low growl sounded behind her and Zane inched closer.

Geoffrey's gaze flew to the other man, but then returned to hers. "We have things to discuss," he said, in that decisive tone he could take.

Harper shook her head. "No. We're not going

anywhere and we have nothing to discuss."

"Your mother would like to see our engagement back on," Geoffrey said quickly. "*I* would like to see our engagement back on."

He expected her to make more promises to him? "*No*," Harper said again. "My mother would like to see me happy, and that won't happen when I'm with you."

Geoffrey's brows drew together. "You belong in San Francisco. Where our families are, where I am, where we go to the museums on Sundays and take in the theater whenever we can."

Take in the theater. How had she not seen how pompous he could be? "I'm not only a museums and theater kind of woman anymore, Geoffrey. I'm different now."

"Nonsense," he said.

"I've kayaked. And paddle boarded. I hope to try whitewater rafting soon," she told him. "I run almost every day."

"You sweat?" he asked, incredulous. "You hate to sweat."

"I *used* to hate to sweat. Now I like to be active and—"

"She gets dirty," Zane put in, his deep voice low but perfectly clear. "She gets dirty with me."

Dirty. A secret shiver trickled down her spine at the innuendo and her head turned to get a glimpse of the big man's face. It looked carved from granite and more than a little bit angry.

"Dirty?" Geoffrey scowled. "For God's sake."

"Dirty," Zane repeated.

"Can you back off, sir?" Geoffrey said, addressing Zane, his eyes narrowed. "This is a conversation for two."

"This is a wholly unnecessary conversation," Harper insisted.

"She's right," Zane said, and his hand came to her shoulder, heavy and hot. "Because we're together now."

Geoffrey's brows shot toward his receding hairline. "What? Harper, you're with this…this Neanderthal?"

The whole diner went silent at that. Eagles's Ridge clearly didn't like a stranger insulting one of their native born sons. Ryder Westbrook, Bailey's boyfriend, shot to his feet and came striding over. "Is there some reason we don't kick this jerk's ass, Z?" he asked.

"I'm trying to think of one," Zane said, conversationally. "Harper doesn't want him here. I sure as hell don't want him here. And he's not taking the hint very well."

Geoffrey ignored the other two men and looked to Harper. "You're the quiet, decorous, always polite woman I've known for the last five years. Nothing's different. You only need to come back home to see that. To *be* that again. To have my ring on your finger once more."

"At your request, she gave you back your damn ring," Zane said and his other hand clapped onto her other shoulder. "And now—I don't know how to make this any clearer, so listen carefully—Harper is with *me*."

Happiness burst like confetti bombs inside her. She glanced up at him again, not bothering to hide a bright smile.

Though Zane didn't take his gaze of Geoffrey's

face, his fingers squeezed, letting her know he'd noticed it. And appreciated it.

"I can't believe this," Geoffrey said, shaking his head. "You'd really hook up with this...this barbarian? You're too delicate, too refined. He won't handle you with enough care—"

"He handles me just fine," she said hotly. "I'm not delicate or decorous, or at least not only those things that you make sound more like an insult than a compliment."

Her ex continued to shake his head. "I don't buy any of this, Harper, you should—"

"No." Her temper spiked and she was suddenly wagging one finger in front of his face. "It doesn't matter what you buy or what you accept or what you think I 'should.' Nothing about you matters, including you not seeing me as who I am and who I'm becoming, because *he* does." She whirled out of Zane's hold in order to face him.

"And I don't need a ring or promises from him," she continued, not looking away from Zane. "Just that one simple thing."

His hard expression softened. "Sweets," he said, reaching for her.

She moved into him at the same time as the diner door swung open again and a cacophony of buzzing sound entered. Both she and Zane looked toward the entrance, where a knot of little kids marched in, blowing enthusiastically on kazoos.

"Uh-oh," Zane said, then put her away from him. "I've got to—"

But what he was going to say was drowned out by a loud, frightening, other-worldly howl. Then came the noise of claws scrabbling on wood and Gambler shot from somewhere at the rear of the diner, entering the main room. Empty chairs were knocked sideways and glasses shattered to the floor as the dog zigged and zagged about the place, around customers and under tables.

Ryder and Zane attempted to corral the agitated dog, but he continued to dodge and weave until finally he made his way to the door. An obliging child opened it despite the shouted "*No!*" from Ryder and Zane. The canine took off like a shot.

Then Gambler's owner sped after him.

Harper looked at Geoffrey, who'd taken refuge behind a rack that held real estate and tourist activities brochures. Then she glanced at Ryder who was looking back at her, a bemused smile on his handsome face. He nodded at her, a clear *go ahead*.

Giving him a grin in return, she went in pursuit of her guy.

Later, Harper and Zane were in his A-frame, Gambler snoring on his bed in the corner. The two humans were snuggled under Zane's comforter on his own bed, skin-to-skin. Her head rested on his shoulder and he toyed with her hair as their heartbeats slowed.

"That wasn't Stella with me this time," Zane said, wrapping a lock around his finger and tugging it a little. "It was all Harper Grace and Harper Grace alone."

A little smile tugged at the corners of her lips. He was right. She'd just been herself and it had been a smashing success. Once they'd managed to contain Gambler—they'd found him in Sentinel Park, barking at a squirrel up a tree—they'd loaded him and themselves into Zane's truck and gone straight to his place. Without a word, he'd led her to the loft and then taken her into his arms for a succession of drugging kisses. From there, it had moved from a slow mutual undressing to a tender exploration of each other's bodies followed up by explosive climaxes.

"Though I think we might classify that as make-up sex," he said.

"Make-up sex?" she asked, lifting her head to look at him, a slight frown bringing her brows together. "Were we in a fight?"

"Not exactly, though I'm a little pissed at you for spending any time at all with that jerk, let alone two years."

Harper sighed and put her cheek back to his chest. "Haven't you ever made a mistake like that...by misreading cues, or making up feelings someone has that aren't really there?"

"All the guys in high school detention made up fantasies about our teacher Miss Woods, aka Miss Woody. Do you mean like that?"

She lifted her head again to stare at him. "Diana? You fantasized about her as teenagers?"

His lips twitched. "Oh, *yeah*. Elaborate, graphic fantasies. That's how she came by the nickname Miss Woody. Get it?"

Harper's eyes rounded. "Boys are very bad," she said primly.

"Men are even worse," he said, his eyes alight with mischief as he ran a callused hand suggestively over her hip. "Give me a few minutes to recover and I'll show you just how much worse we can be."

At that, she couldn't help smiling at him, happiness bursting like more confetti bombs inside and all around her.

He smiled back. Then he sobered. "I did make a real mistake like you're describing once, though. Years ago, when I was young and dumb."

"Oh?" Harper remembered Jane telling her Zane had been hurt by a girl. She sat up, half on her hip, and held the sheet to her chest.

"She was a pretty thing, a real Southern belle, and I wanted to give her everything I had and more. I even fancied that she was as infatuated with me as I was with her."

"You weren't in love with her, just infatuated?" Somehow she liked the thought of that better.

"Young and dumb, remember? It was definitely infatuation. I was away from home for the first time and very susceptible to stupid."

"How did it end?"

"I'd like to claim I smartened up, but what really happened was she told me I was too rough and too tough for the expensive furniture in her parents' home not to mention I was no match for her fragile femininity, and then she broke up with me."

"Poor Zane." Harper ran the back of her fingers over the stubble on his jaw. "Though rough and tough doesn't sound like much of a slur."

"Not to me anymore either. Not when a beautiful woman stood in a crowded diner and claimed I handled her delicate and decorous self just fine."

Harper felt her face redden. "I did that, didn't I? In front of everybody."

Zane grinned. "It was great. But only half as great as the next thing you said to that jerk ex of yours."

Nothing about you matters, including you not seeing me as who I am and who I'm becoming, because he *does.*

"I meant it, Zane," she said now. "All of it."

And I don't need a ring or promises from him. Just that one simple thing.

"I know, sweets," he said, and the serious expression on his face made her heart jolt and every inch of her skin flush with heat.

She swallowed, trying to think of something to say that wouldn't betray how much she was beginning to feel for him. This was supposed to stay casual, after all.

But he beat her to it, taking the moment from tender to naughty just by plucking the sheet from her fingers to reveal her bare breasts.

"And now I think it's time I made an honest pair of us by proving just exactly how dirty you can get with me," he said, tweaking one nipple.

It instantly peaked and a jolt of heat shot to the soft place between her legs. "Well, I could use some more training," she said, already going breathless. "Especially because there's something I've always wanted to get really, really good at."

Then she dived beneath the covers, gratified by his instant groan when her hands and mouth found that he had, indeed, recovered.

Chapter 10

The Thursday night before the weekend of the mud run was the by-invitation-only, "soft" opening of Bailey Tucker's new restaurant, Blue Moon. Harper hadn't hesitated to agree to attend with Zane. Not only couldn't she wait to get a good look inside the place, but there was also the expected arrival of the mother of the Tucker siblings. Zane said she'd promised to show during the cocktail hour before the meal slated to be served to friends and family.

They drove together in his truck in what she considered to be a contented silence. Despite his busy schedule at A To Z and her list-upon-list of what had to be accomplished before the library charity event on Sunday morning, they'd managed to see each other, talk on the phone, and even sleep in the same bed a few times—with exciting before-sleep activities that left her sated and feeling closer to him than she'd ever felt with anyone.

Still, she was careful to keep her expectations at a

minimum and not take their growing relationship too seriously. After all, she'd promised.

But she'd bought a new dress in that cute boutique Jane had introduced her to before her date night. It was sapphire blue, fitted at the top with a fairly short A-line skirt. The neckline reached to her throat, but the shoulders and elbow-length sleeves were in a lace of the same deep-blue shade, which allowed her skin to peek through the delicate design.

Now she smoothed the hem lower on her thighs, and held out one foot to admire her new nude pumps.

"Did I say you make my mouth water tonight?" Zane asked.

Pleasure warmed her all over. "Thank you." She touched her up-do, not fussy or smooth, but not messy either. It had taken the stylist an hour to get the look just right. "You're no slouch either."

Understatement, of course. He looked unbelievably hot in dark slacks, dress shoes, and a black-and-gray checked sports jacket over a black dress shirt, the collar unbuttoned. "Is it okay to go without a tie?"

"Adam and I told Bailey that if she made this a noose-only place, we'd refuse to step foot inside it."

"You would never refuse," Harper protested. She couldn't imagine the brothers denying their sister anything.

"We wouldn't," Zane agreed, sending her a smile. "But the dress code doesn't include a tie requirement anyway."

They turned along another road, and Harper admired the way the last of the day's sunlight filtered through the trees. Eagle's Ridge was nothing like the city that she came from, but it had beauties and charms that were unrivaled.

"Everything in place for the mud run?" Zane asked.

"I think so." Her belly tightened a little at the thought of what lie ahead on Sunday. "I have a remarkable young man who's taken it on as his Eagle Scout service project. He has a future ahead in logistics, I'm just sure. Plus, he's gotten the local Boy and Girl Scout troops to volunteer to help as well as the Friends of the Library team."

"I'll be there too," Zane said. "Ready to do whatever you need. Adam, Ryder, and Wyatt will be on hand as well."

She beamed at him but reminded herself it wasn't just for her—that he and his brother and friends were going to be supporting the community too. "Thanks," she said.

Her breath caught as they pulled into the parking lot of Blue Moon. "Oh." She clasped her hands together as she caught sight of the impressive stone building with its wide mullioned windows. She knew behind it was a patio overlooking the river, but the front was spectacular too. In the gathering dusk, fairy lights sparkled in the trees and were wrapped around wine barrels filled with flowers that flanked the path to the deep porch and double front doors.

Harper almost felt like a celebrity on a red carpet as she walked up the flagstone route, her hand tucked into Zane's elbow. Apparently Bailey had hired a photographer for the night—maybe to capture images for her website?—and as directed, she found herself smiling for the camera.

The restaurant's interior was both elegant and inviting. Bailey was there to greet them in a long, figure-hugging dress, a midnight black that set off her lovely blonde hair. Ryder stood at her side, at ease in a dark suit and tie.

Zane didn't hesitate to tease him about that last sartorial element, shaking his head and saying it was clear evidence that Ryder was wrapped around his sister's little finger.

They moved farther inside to make room for more arriving guests and found Adam and Jane standing beside a charcuterie table. A server came by with a tray of filled champagne glasses. The bubbles tickled Harper's nose, but the cool, dry taste was delicious as it slid down her throat.

Of course the brothers complained about the dearth of beer.

Zane's arm came around her waist and tucked her close to his side.

Maybe it was the champagne. Maybe it was seeing everyone dressed in their best. But suddenly Harper's stomach was jittering and the room seemed to spin a little.

She put her hand to Zane's waist, steadying herself. He looked down. "Hey, are you okay?" he asked.

His blue-green eyes only made her more dizzy. "I'm good," she lied, even as her body trembled.

"You're ice-cold," he said, rubbing his hand up and down her arm. "Are you sure—"

"I'm fine," she told him, and stepped free of his hold to set her champagne flute aside. "Just..." There wasn't a cogent explanation that she could share. Her sixth sense was suddenly nagging at her, though, setting her on edge, warning her that something big, something life-changing, was hovering over her and was no more than two breaths away from descending.

As if this nervousness was catching, a nearby server stumbled, losing one of the empty glasses on his tray. It landed with a loud shatter, hushing the crowd. Then Zane hurried over to the obviously mortified waiter. "Let me help, man. I'm an expert at crashes and clean-ups."

Everybody laughed and went back to their conversations. Harper's gaze followed the big man as he bent with a linen napkin in hand and scooped up the broken shards.

"That was handled neatly," Ryder said, coming up beside Harper. "Unlike the situation in No Man's Land the other day. Gambler broke three plates, knocked a picture off the wall, and two burgers landed face-down on the floor."

Harper grimaced. "We left you behind with all that." She hadn't seen the other man since she'd run out after Zane and his dog.

"And you also left me behind with…Godfrey, was it?"

"Geoffrey." Her lips twitched. "But you can refer to him as Godfrey if you like."

"I plan on not referring to him ever again," Ryder pledged, a smile in his eyes. "But I'll let you know it took a little physical persuasion to send him on his way."

"Wait. What?"

But Ryder's gaze suddenly shifted and his whole body went on alert. "Excuse me, but I've got to get to Bailey. She's here."

She meaning the mother of the Tucker siblings, Harper realized. Tori Remington who had been Vicky Tucker when she'd lived in Eagle's Ridge. From across the room, Harper stared. The beautiful woman swept into the space, wearing a dramatic gown of amethyst chiffon with jewels of the same color swinging from her ears. Her charisma could be felt even from this distance and it was almost surreal to see in real life the woman she'd watched on a TV screen time and time again.

Bailey greeted her mother with a hug and then she drew Ryder toward the older woman. Adam and Zane joined their circle next, and the reunion appeared cordial if not exactly enthusiastic.

Then Zane looked around and caught her eye only to beckon her forward. Harper took careful steps to join him.

"This is my friend Harper Grace," he told his mother. "She's the librarian in Eagle's Ridge."

His friend. She smiled through the aftermath of that small sting, shaking hands and engaging in some practiced Nob Hill chit chat with the actress. But of course she and Zane were friends, Harper reminded herself. Their relationship was casual.

She'd promised.

Soon they were called to take their seats. Zane led her to a beautifully set table and held her chair, just as he'd done on their first date. His rough fingertips caressed her bare nape as she adjusted her seat. Then he took the neighboring place and others joined them—Adam, Jane, Wyatt, Bailey, Ryder, and Tori Remington.

At another table sat the four founders of Eagle's Ridge with the generation that followed them, including Sam and Brenda. She hadn't seen that couple interact with Zane's mother, but she remembered hearing that Tori/Vicki and the diner manager had been best friends once upon a time.

Then her attention was taken by Bailey, who tapped a fork to her wineglass. When the room quieted, she explained the menu and her philosophy. Farm-to-table organic foods with a French flair that included favorite dishes of both the Westbrook and the Tucker families. That night she'd given a nod to the most popular items on the menu at Veronica's, the restaurant housed previously in the building, re-imagining them for their enjoyment.

The food was beyond delicious and the guests enthusiastic in their praise. As the meal wore on, Harper's earlier sense of imminent disaster moved off. Zane held a succulent bite of lamb to her mouth and she stared into his smiling eyes as she slid it from his fork with her lips. His thigh pressed against hers beneath the table and she felt again that seductive, sweet intimacy.

That warm feeling went beyond just the two of them, though. As a newcomer to Eagle's Ridge, she'd wondered how long it would take to feel part of the community—and right now she did. Adam wisecracked some joking aside to his brother and Zane laughed and Jane shared with her a happy look that made Harper feel on the inside of the Tucker family too. Accepted and liked, a feeling underlined when Bailey brushed her shoulder in a friendly gesture as she refilled Harper's wineglass herself.

The meal ended with a decadent tasting plate of small desserts and an espresso that Bailey referred to as Café Gourmand. After savoring their last bites and final sips of coffee, Harper and Zane were not the first and not the last to take their leave. Bailey glowed with satisfaction as they delivered additional and sincere compliments followed by their affectionate goodbyes.

They both were silent on the ride home until Zane pronounced, "She's going to be a huge success."

Harper smiled. "I completely agree."

"It's her dream," Zane added, his own grin white in the dark interior of the cab. "And she went for it."

"I think that might be a Tucker trait," Harper said. "Isn't A To Z the same for you? And the adventure camp for troubled kids Adam's dream?"

"Yeah," he said, his tone thoughtful. "That's so."

His hand was warm on hers as he walked her to her condo. "As much as I'd like to stay the night, sweets, I'm going into the office extra early tomorrow and juggling like crazy to free up my Sunday for you."

To free up my Sunday for you.

"I understand," she said, using her key to open her door. She hesitated on the threshold and turned to him, automatically tilting up her face for his kiss.

Instead of immediately accepting the unspoken invitation, he stared down at her, a little smile curving his mouth.

His masculine beauty dizzied her again and the stars overhead seemed to reel in the sky. She was close enough to feel his heat and she wanted to rub against it, she wanted to imprint herself on him, so he would always, always…be hers.

Be hers.

Oh, no. This deep, now undeniable longing was what she'd been dreading acknowledging all evening. The disaster that had been hovering over her head.

At the realization, her heart jolted in her chest and her blood slowed as a chill fell over her. God. There was nothing casual about what she felt for him, nothing casual at all. She was in love. She was completely in love with Zane Tucker.

But she'd made that promise to keep things casual!

And she'd failed, hadn't she? Her feelings for him had slid straight into serious territory.

She was in love with the man who rescued goofy dogs and who empowered shy librarians. She was in love with a man who loved his country and his family and gave them all he had. This honest, honorable man, who she could treat with no less honor and no less honesty.

"Zane," she said, and her voice sounded unlike her, rough and scratchy. Her eyes stung and she blinked to keep the tears at bay.

"Sweets?"

Sweets. So, so sweet.

She stepped back and gripped the edge of the door, ready to swing it shut. "I can't do this anymore," she whispered.

"What?"

"I can't keep my promise. I can't be casual about this any longer. About us. And it will break me if I pretend otherwise, if I try to continue on this way."

He stared, clearly dumbfounded.

"I...goodbye," she croaked out, and shut the door in his face.

Saturday afternoon, in a murderous temper that had been brewing since late Thursday night, Zane stomped through the back door of No Man's Land. Just to make a crap couple of days even crappier, a last-minute cancellation left him with some free hours.

When all he wanted was to stay so busy he didn't

have time to think.

Or feel.

But he didn't have any effing feelings, he told himself. At least not the kind that got all weepy and whiny just because some woman decided she didn't want to see him anymore. Stuff like that didn't faze Zane Tucker, not when his relationships were always of the temporary variety.

That he'd been blindsided by the librarian breaking it off was no big deal.

Really. It shouldn't bother him at all. He was an easygoing kind of guy. Everybody said so.

He marched into the kitchen, hoping to find a burger and fries already plated up that he could liberate from whatever patron they were intended for. His dad would only need to slap another patty on the grill to satisfy the customer.

And Zane was in no mood to wait.

Sam glanced over his shoulder as he expertly flipped some sizzling meat. Then his eyes widened. "You okay, Son? You look a bit…rough around the edges."

"I *am* rough around the edges," Zane said, but automatically ran his hand over his bristly chin. If he'd been still seeing Harper, he'd keep to a smooth shave so as not to mar her soft, tender skin.

But he wasn't still seeing Harper.

A plate sat under the warming lights on the pass-through. A chicken sandwich would have to do, and the fries looked hot and crisp.

"I'm taking this Dad," he said, and grabbed the food.

His father sighed and moved to the refrigerator to snag another breaded chicken breast. "If Mandy was doing her job right, that meal would already be delivered to the table."

Leaning against the counter by the sink, Zane wolfed down a late lunch. Then he set the plate aside and poured himself milk into a pebbled plastic glass that he drained in one go.

Sam glanced over at him again. "You still look ready to strangle a grizzly with your bare hands. Do you want to talk about it?"

"No." What would he say? He had no right to be pissed at Harper for being truthful.

I can't be casual about this any longer.

Casual was his choice. The way he'd wanted to conduct their relationship, the same as with the other women in his past. When that no longer worked for her, then she was right to end things.

It will break me if I continue this way.

At the thought of Harper being broken, that he might have a hand in hurting her, his rage erupted. His arm came up and he threw the plastic glass into the stainless steel sink with such force that it shattered like an egg.

"Son." Sam moved away from the grill, his expression concerned, and dragged out a chair from the breakroom. "Sit down. Tell me what's going on."

Zane dropped onto the seat and hung his head, his hands in his hair. After a few slow breaths he felt marginally calmer. "I'm okay," he said, looking up to meet his father's gaze. "I'll be all right."

"I'm here to listen."

"Thanks, Dad." Zane pushed his hands through his hair another time. "But...there's no words." He couldn't explain to himself why he was so angry. So frustrated too. It wasn't with Harper. It was because…hell, he just didn't know.

"I have something to say, then." Sam built a burger, then slid it onto a plate, put the plate on the pass-through. "It's about me and Brenda."

Zane straightened, glad for the distraction. "Yeah, Dad?" He was pretty certain he knew where this was going. His father was about to confess he was dating the diner manager. He'd heard from Adam who'd heard from Jane that Sam had invited Brenda to the house to have dinner and spend the night.

That last part he tried very hard not to think about.

"I'm moving in with her," Sam said.

Blinking, Zane felt his mouth drop. "Huh?"

"It makes sense," his dad continued. "We'll start our lives together in her place. She moved there after her husband died, so there's no ghosts. Not like at our house."

"But…" Surprise stole Zane's words.

"It's time I get out of my rut, as Brenda has been telling me."

"Grandpa Max lives there," Zane pointed out, still trying to absorb the news.

"And he can stay on in the apartment over the garage or go back to his house once it's repaired. You know how he likes his own space. He won't be sorry to live alone again."

"Do you…does she…" He shook his head, still amazed by the changes his father was proposing.

"I love her," Sam said simply. "She loves me. The past is behind us and we want a future together. And we want that future to start right now. As a matter of fact, we're looking at the calendar to determine when we'll become husband and wife."

Husband and wife? Zane blinked again, trying to take in this next piece of information. *Really?* He opened his mouth, about to gently suggest they slow the Sam-and-Brenda train down a little, but then he recalled what Harper once told him. *A man who really wants to marry someone should want to settle on a date right away.*

"Well." Zane got to his feet to man-hug his dad, adding a bone-jolting slap to his back. "I'm happy for you, Dad."

And he was, now that he was getting more accustomed to the idea. Happy for Brenda too. "Where is the lucky lady? I'd like to offer her my best wishes."

Sam nodded toward the pass-through. "At a table in the corner."

Craning his neck, Zane indeed saw Brenda, sitting with a mug in front of her. Across from his mother.

He looked back at his dad. "She's still here?"

"For a couple more days, from what I understand. You should go out and say hello."

Beyond the brief and superficial conversation he'd had with his mother at Bailey's soft opening, he'd not seen her or exchanged additional words with her. Engrossed in work and wrapped up in his bad mood, he'd actually not given her another thought.

If he had, he'd guess she'd been hanging with Bailey. Adam certainly hadn't mentioned her.

But now she was inside No Man's Land, with Brenda. Though that wasn't so very weird, was it? Years ago, they'd been good friends. Good enough friends, he supposed now—hoped so, anyway—that his mother didn't begrudge a new chapter of life for her ex-husband and the woman he'd worked alongside for so many years.

"Go on, Son," Sam counseled, in that dad tone of voice that was impossible to ignore. "It will be good for both of you."

As Zane approached the two women, Brenda rose from her seat. She'd done something to her hair, it was much shorter now and framed her face. But Zane guessed the new youthfulness he sensed about her was due more to the joy she'd found with Sam than a hairdresser's scissors.

Way to go, Brenda.

"Hey." He kissed her cheek as she passed him on her path to the kitchen. "Welcome to the family."

That brought a sheen of tears to her eyes.

He recalled the same in Harper's Thursday night when she'd dumped him and felt another flood of...whatever it was. He ruthlessly tamped it down, though, and continued to his mother. She watched carefully as he lowered into the chair across from her.

"Zane," she said, inclining her head.

"Mom." He studied her face, unsurprised to find she looked older, but just as beautiful in the natural light of day. "You're still in town."

"I have a suite at the Broadleaf. I'm going home Monday morning, but I want to be with Bailey at Blue Moon during its first weekend."

"I'm sure she appreciates that."

His mother glanced down at her mug, her hand turning it in idle circles. "I have considered stopping at A To Z Watersports, but I wasn't sure of my welcome."

Zane shrugged. "You should come by if you can make the time. It's no fancy farm-to-table restaurant, but Adam and I like it. It's the perfect business for us."

She glanced up at him now, a small smile curving her mouth. "I'm so glad. I always said you'd get everything you wanted."

"Yeah." Even when he'd been struggling for his next breath, she'd been certain, so *he'd* been certain. "Thanks for that."

"I know I hurt you, though, by leaving. That I was selfish—"

"Let's not go there." He didn't say it to be kind, he said it because it was all so long ago he saw no point in raking through the old pain. The anger he'd felt then had no place in his present.

"All right." His mother nodded, then sipped from her mug, set it down again. "I enjoyed meeting your friend the other night. Though I'm supposing Harper's a little more that."

He was already shaking his head. "It's not going to work out between us."

"I'm sorry to hear that."

"I'm not the right guy for her," he found himself telling his mother. "I've always been a man not interested in settling down—I just don't see myself that way. And she deserves more. A forever type who'll be all that that means."

"And you aren't one of those forever types?"

"Nope, like I said, I just don't see myself that way." He linked his hands on the table. "I'm going to be the bachelor uncle. The ice guy."

His mom tilted her head. "The what?"

"You know. The guy who's only trusted to brings bags of ice to the holiday bashes. Maybe a dozen rolls or two if I really prove myself."

She laughed. He suddenly recalled that sound, the lightness of it and how it had once filled their old house. "That doesn't sound like much to look forward to."

"It's who I am." He shrugged. "How I've always been."

"That doesn't mean you can't change, Zane. Be different. You can change your plans for yourself and what your future might be."

As his dad would say, get out of his rut? But he shook his head again. "No. I—"

"Take it from me," his mother said, reaching across the table to touch her fingertips to the back of his hand. "Things might turn out different than you expect. Sometimes a dream drags you forward, right out of your comfort zone."

Sunday morning, Zane woke when it was still dark. He stared in the direction of the ceiling and for the first time felt the silence of his house as oppressive. Not to mention lonely. The A-frame could use more laughter, he thought. A softer touch. A woman's voice.

Echoes of her voice and of her perfume.

He jackknifed up, eager to get away from that uncomfortable notion. At the first thump of his feet to the floor, Gambler came awake, shaking and dancing and communicating his impatience for breakfast with a cold nose in the cup of Zane's palm.

The dog scrambled down the stairs ahead of him and then ran circles in the kitchen, his tail sweeping the pencil sharpener off the low desk. "Whoa, boy," Zane said, as always amazed by his dog's unceasing energy. It was incredible how this bundle of furred mania and odd panics could quiet when around books and little Bella.

The child's presence calmed him and it seemed, with her, he'd found his canine purpose.

Not unlike the peace Zane had found with Harper. He'd slept in her library and on her couch, both unprecedented. Things he'd never shared with his twin—about his hapless romance with the Southern belle and about the guilt he'd felt when his mother left—he'd revealed to Harper. He'd never let down his guard like that with any other woman.

Then there was that bookmark he continued carrying around like a talisman. Why couldn't he let it go?

Why didn't he want to let *her* go?

Because she's your *purpose*, a voice inside him said. *Your purpose is to make Harper happy. To be that forever man she deserves.*

"I can't," he said aloud, alarmed by the concept. His mouth dried and his stomach went queasy. "Even if I wanted to, I'm not—"

Sometimes a dream drags you forward. His mother's voice echoed in his head now. *Right out of your comfort zone.*

You can change your plans for yourself and what your future might be.

Change. That damn word that had been plaguing him for weeks. He didn't want to, damn it—or more precisely, he didn't think he could. Nobody had ever considered him husband material before and that's what Harper Grace deserved…a man who could be soft when she needed him to be. A man who could be gentle. Everybody knew Zane was that bull in a china shop only guaranteed to break things.

Later, still troubled by his early morning thoughts, he met his brother, Ryder, and Wyatt at the staging center for the mud run, just on the outskirts of Sentinel Park. Though they did some heavy lifting—cases of water, boxes of first aid supplies—all looked to be in readiness for the nine o'clock start time. Kudos to the Eagle Scout-in-the-making and particularly the volunteers from the fire department. They'd designed and built the mud-and-obstacle course on a vast tract of cleared county land that usually stored heavy machinery as well as supplies for road and sewer repair.

What he didn't see was any sign of Harper, even when there was a mere hour to go before the runners were to set off. Had she decided not to participate after all?

He was standing beside Wyatt, both of them dressed in athletic wear and with their contestant numbers pinned to their shirts, when the sassy swing of a ponytail caught his eye.

Half-turning, he saw her twenty-five yards away, her head bent over a clipboard, dressed in running tights and a matching long-sleeved runner's tee. Someone walked by and paused to have a word with her. She looked up at the person, smiled.

And Zane felt that heart he'd always supposed to be as hard and unmovable as the rest of him tumble down to his toes, then bounce up to his throat, before settling behind his ribs once again, beating there at a frantic, urgent pace.

It was then that the truth that had been swirling around him all morning—hell, probably since she'd shut the door in his face Thursday night—finally penetrated his stubborn brain.

He was in love.

He was in love with Harper Grace.

That's what it meant, the peace he experienced when he was around her, the purpose he felt compelled to pursue—her happiness—the anticipation rising inside him as he imagined explaining this to her and persuading her into his arms once again.

Would she believe he wanted a forever with her now? Because, so help him, he did. Badly.

It was a change, sure, but change was in the air, and if Bailey could do it, and Adam, and even his dad and Brenda, then Zane was going after what he now wanted too.

"You are *gone* for that woman," Wyatt said. "Don't even bother lying to me about it."

Zane looked over at his friend. "I—" he began, ready to deny the charge.

But he never wanted to lie about that, he realized. To himself, to anyone. "I do," he told Wyatt, his heart still beating wildly. The sun seemed to shine brighter and the trees and sky bombarded him with an extra dose of beauty. "God help me, I really do."

"Then you owe me," the other man said. "And I have spent some time considering my end of the wager. As a matter of fact, I've struck upon the perfect thing."

Uh-oh. Wyatt's oh-so-cheerful expression didn't give Zane a good feeling in his gut.

It only got worse when the man shared the exact price Zane would have to pay for falling in love.

Protest was compulsory, because hell, it was just too much to expect. "Damn it, Wyatt, come on—"

The former SEAL crossed his arms over his chest. "A bet is a bet."

A bet is a bet. Words Zane had lived by, and might possibly die of humiliation by. "Fine, whatever." Still, he glared at his friend. "If this causes me to permanently lose the girl, I personally guarantee your next career move will be to Seattle's Woodland Park Zoo, where you'll be elephant shit scooper-in-chief."

Harper's nerves were strung to the breaking point as she walked about the mud run staging area checking on the final last minute details. Not only did she want the event to be a success for the library, but she'd realized it was also a testing ground for her ability to remain in Eagle's Ridge. Thanks to all that needed to be accomplished in the last couple of days, she'd had plenty of reasons to remain holed up in her office. But today she'd be forced to face community members, new friends, and Zane's family.

She wasn't entirely sure, but maybe even Zane himself.

If that hurt too much, if knowing she could never have him as her own was going to make every day in Eagle's Ridge a misery, then she was going to have to move on.

In the middle of a sleepless night, alone in her bed and remembering his every touch, his every word, his smile, she'd struck upon the idea that the mud run would be her trial. The four miles of mud and obstacles were sure to exact a physical and emotional toll—because her determination to participate came straight back to Zane, after all—but if she could cross the finish line on her own, then she was strong enough to stay in this town even when he moved on to some other woman.

In a place so small, she'd be sure to hear about it. See it.

Just the thought ripped a tear in her heart, but maybe she could find the inner strength to carry on. This morning she'd find out.

Now it was time to gather near the starting line, with its wide banner declaring *Get Dirty for Books!* She handed off her clipboard to Josh, the almost-Eagle Scout, and took a place at the very back. Though she'd considered saying a few words before the "gun" went off—they'd be using the siren function on a megaphone—she left that to the mayor and the fire chief.

Mayor Warren thanked the hundreds of participants and the dozens of volunteers. The fire chief explained where to find the aid stations, urged participants not to push too hard, especially those young, old, and new to physical endurance trials. After that he led them all in a pledge, making them repeat they understood that the event was "a challenge, not a race." "Teamwork" and "partnerships," he told them, were more important than individual achievement this Sunday morning.

Then the siren blasted and the crowd began to move.

From her position at the very back, Harper and the knot of participants around her at first could only manage a slow jog. Caught as she was amongst them, she really couldn't see what was in store and mostly worked on managing to avoid the elbows of the people on either side of her and trying not to step on the heels of the person directly in front of her as they climbed a substantial hill.

Still, the incline and her lingering nerves had her

breathing hard as she breached the top. The woman beside her was panting too, and she gave Harper a sidelong look. "It gets harder than this," she said. "I hope I don't embarrass myself."

"Yeah, me…" Then her words trailed off as the ground fell away below them and they could see what lay ahead.

Yellow flags, the small ones like landscapers used, delineated the snaking path that led from obstacle to obstacle. She saw muddy ponds of water, low hills, a maze of old tires hanging from chains. Then a couple more ponds, these topped with lines of "razor wire"—she'd been told it was actually flexible and rubber covered—that would require participants to bend or crawl, followed by wooden walls with long ropes flung over them to aid in climbing. More mud. More water. Balance beams across even more rectangles of sludgy water. Hay, piled twenty feet high would be interesting to scale when one was damp and dirty. Beyond them, metal culverts were half-buried and would require more crawling and ducking.

She exchanged a look with the other woman. "Fun?"

Her companion lifted her hand, inviting a high-five. "Let's get dirty for books!"

And then they set off, their pace still impeded by the crowd ahead. But they persisted, encouraged by the volunteers and spectators milling about the space, yet staying well clear of the inevitable muddy arcs of water as people ran, stumbled, and fell in the process of moving through, up, over, or down what was put in their way.

Harper quickly understood where her training had been incomplete. While the actual one-foot-in-front-of-the-other was doable, she should have also worked on her upper body strength. On the first wooden wall she was expected to mount, she stalled, her hands slipping on the rope that was supposed to aid her way.

Disappointment and frustration made her scowl. She couldn't give up so easily. Then she felt a hand on her behind, boosting her up. "C'mon, you can do it."

She glanced over her shoulder to meet distinctive blue-green eyes, and for a moment her heart squeezed and her grip went slack. That hand gave another push and she realized it was Adam, not Zane, who was behind her. With renewed determination, she scrambled upward, and upon reaching the top was able to give him a breathless "Thanks."

He smiled, its similarity to his brother's giving her heart another quick wring. "You okay?"

His kindness made her nose sting and she blinked away hot tears. "Great," she mumbled.

"I'll watch you climb down," he said gently. "Go slow. It'll be okay, I promise."

Why did that sound like he referred to something else? she wondered, as she picked her way to the bottom, using the 2 x 4 footholds provided.

Then Adam was passing her, with a pat on the back and a quick wink. "Keep an eye out for my brother."

Oh, no, she groaned silently. That meant he was here, didn't it? But she wasn't going to be looking for him. She was going to keep her head down and cross the finish line without giving him another thought.

Okay, she thought of him a dozen times as she struggled along the route. Nerves jangling, worried that any moment she might come across him, she stumbled and fell face first in a waist-high vat of thick mud. Chagrined, she clambered to her feet, rivulets of wet dirt oozing off of her, and was grateful to find a firefighter once she climbed out who had a hose in hand, ready to spray clean water. She closed her eyes as he rinsed her down and only opened them to see Bailey standing nearby, Gambler on a leash at her side.

The other woman waved gaily and gave her a big thumbs-up. Harper responded with a weak one of her own, and then trudged ahead, refusing to feel humiliated.

She was going to do this. She was going to survive the mud run.

She was going to survive a broken heart.

Now she didn't look to either side. Her focus was trained straight ahead and her attention solely on the next task. She belly-crawled through metal tubes, she spit hay from her mouth after scaling the top of that hill and sliding down the other side, she slogged through a muddy maze of low wooden structures.

The finish line finally came in sight.

More spectators lined the path and those participants already finished were gathered near tents where she knew volunteers were prepared to hand out juice, coffee, tea, and a variety of healthy and not-so-healthy foodstuffs. Her stomach roiled at the thought of eating and she paused, trying to calm it, which only allowed the muscles in her legs to turn to lead.

Harper closed her eyes. *Must. Make. It.*

The onlookers were suddenly shouting encouragement and laughing, but she didn't have the energy to determine what that was all about. Instead she plodded forward, her gaze on the last two obstacles—a series of parallel balance beams set over another long, rectangular tank of mud, and then a final wall. Her heart fell to her belly as she studied that one. While it wasn't as tall as another she'd managed that day, it had a lip like a skateboarding halfpipe. Watching others ahead of her, she could see it required people to get a running start in order to make it over that curve, or else they'd slide right back to the bottom.

"One challenge at a time," a voice advised. A familiar voice. Zane. "Don't get worried about the next until you do the one right in front of you."

She didn't dare look at him, even though his very presence gave her the incentive to move. Head down, she hurried to a balance beam. Stepped onto it.

This should be doable, she thought. She had narrow feet. *Just walk, heel-to-toe.*

Miracle of miracles, she managed, even though she was wholly aware that Zane was traversing a neighboring balance beam, moving at her same speed. Still, she didn't look at him, even when she wobbled and from the corner of her eye saw his hand shoot out, ready to steady her. Ignoring it, she made it all the way across on her own.

"Way to go, Harper," he said, warm with praise. "I knew you could do it."

Could she? Could she really? Spend her life in Eagle's Ridge bumping up against Zane Tucker on mud runs or in the diner or maybe when he came to check out another Western novel?

Rather than responding, she continued onward, that daunting obstacle up ahead. Zane passed her, she felt the air whoosh by her as the big man moved, but her vision narrowed to a tunnel as she pulled air into her lungs.

She was so tired. Quitting didn't sound so bad.

She couldn't believe she would ever get over him anyway.

Someone yelled her name and she turned her head to see Bailey and Gambler keeping stride—slow, deliberate—along with her. "Go, Harper!" the other woman called out. "Just a little bit more!"

Unable to dredge up even a smile, her gaze swung back to the obstacle ahead. And then there was nothing to do but gather her flagging power and make a run for it.

Halfway up, she slid down the slick muddied surface.

The second time, she didn't even make it that far.

At the bottom, she bent over, her hands on her knees, trying to breathe. A third attempt seemed impossible.

"Harper!" Zane again.

Nearly ready to admit defeat, she raised her eyes in the direction of his voice. He straddled the top of the lipped wall, and his arm reached down in her direction. "Try again, sweets, and I'll catch you."

Instead, she backed away. "I have to do it myself," she whispered.

"What's that?" His face was smeared with mud and his clothes too. They seemed to be ripped...or something. Her brain was tired like the rest of her and couldn't figure it out, not even the odd band circling his head.

He bent to stretch his arm farther. "Harper, come on baby, try it again. I'm here for you."

But he wouldn't be there for her even if she made it over the stupid thing and it sparked her temper for some absurd reason. She glared at him, and decided it was better than crying. "I need to do it alone," she yelled up at him. "All by myself."

An expression crossed his face that she couldn't interpret. "No, baby. Not ever again. Never by yourself again. Harper, I love you."

She stared at him in shock.

"I do, baby. I'm in love with you." His hand beckoned her. "Now let me help you over this last hurdle and we can talk about it."

Something tickled the back of her neck. Maybe it was drying mud, but she looked around and realized the pair of them were the center of attention, spectators and volunteers alike standing around, apparently riveted by their little drama.

Her anger spiked again, her other emotions so tangled she couldn't sort through how she felt about his public declaration or even if she could believe in it. If she *should* believe in it.

It hurt so much to love and to trust.

Pushed now by her renewed temper, she backed up from the curved wooden wall. *Do it, Harper*, she told herself, and made another run at it. Momentum propelled her forward and her feet scrambled higher than ever before. Her breath caught, elation sang in her blood. *Almost there!*

Then she felt herself begin to slide.

No, no, no, she thought, tears once again stinging her eyes. But she could see that outstretched hand in front of her. Large, male, strong.

"Take it," Zane commanded, his tone urgent.

And instinct won out over caution. Her fingers wrapped his and his grip—as solid as the rest of him—hauled her the last crucial distance.

Now they both straddled the top, face-to-face.

Dirty and breathing hard, they looked into each other's eyes.

"You didn't have to say that, you know," Harper managed to get out.

"Say what?"

She glanced away. "That 'I love you' business." It had taken her a moment, but now she understood why he'd said such a thing. "I appreciate you thought it was a motivation—"

"I said it because it's true."

Her gaze jerked to his. "No…"

"Yes." Though they were dangling on the top of the wooden wall, he didn't seem inclined to move. Nor lower his voice. "I don't want our relationship to be casual either."

Other participants were attempting the ascent on either side of them, but they might as well be ants as far as Harper was concerned. "I didn't think you wanted to be serious."

One corner of his mouth lifted. "I didn't. But then a pretty librarian came into my life and made me see things differently. See myself differently. She made me want different things too."

"Me?" she asked, still disbelieving.

"You." He fished in his muddy garments and from somewhere withdrew a small scrap of fabric, lifting it for her to see.

"My bookmark." She reached for it, but he quickly tucked it away again.

"I've been carrying it around like a boy with a lock of his sweetheart's hair," Zane said with a crooked smile. "I guess it proves I have a soft side after all."

Her throat tightened as she tried to take this in.

"Are you...are you saying you're the leopard that changed its spots?"

"*You* changed them, Harper." His gaze intensified. "Do you believe me?"

She couldn't think, not when he was looking at her like that. She could only feel a sweet, sweet surge of joy. "I...yes."

"Then take me," Zane said, his mesmerizing eyes filling her vision. "Say you'll be mine."

Be his? Oh, it was such a tempting, delicious idea, if only she could truly believe in it. To be Zane's woman, to live life within the protective circle of his arms. Harper swayed toward him.

Zane reached for her. "Say you'll be mine and then we'll complete this damn run together."

Complete this damn run together. Her spine snapped straight, putting distance between them again, as she remembered she'd come here to Eagle's Ridge to change her spots too. To not be protected, cocooned, or coddled. To live with more zest.

To prove that she could, she wanted to, no, *needed to*, cross that finish line alone.

Then they'd see what they might be.

So instead of speaking, she slithered down the other side and started off once more. Her noodle legs didn't help much, but she kept at it, aware that Zane was right behind her.

Ready to pick her up if she fell, she had no doubt.

Her steps faltered at the thought. *She had no doubt.*

But that revelation was to be examined later, and she lowered her head and began to jog. People were clapping and calling her name and she felt a new power growing inside her the closer she came to that line.

Almost there.

Why it happened next, she didn't know. Perhaps it was one of the volunteers, eager to encourage her that last small distance, who picked up the megaphone and let out another earsplitting siren blast. It was followed by an unearthly howl, shouts, Harper thought she heard Bailey's voice, and then someone was yelling Zane's name. She turned in time to see the big man bowled over by his dog, the animal shoving his owner flat to his face in mud before fleeing beyond the finish line.

Zane lay there as if stunned, or dead.

Harper's heart slammed against her ribs. She ran back to bend over him. "Zane!" she choked out his name, alarmed by his stillness and afraid she wouldn't survive if he did not. "Are you all right?"

His head slowly lifted. He blinked up at her. "Just…just the wind. Knocked. Out of me."

Relief rushed through her and she clasped her muddy hands beneath her chin. "Are you sure?"

"Go." He coughed. And she knew he understood how important it was for her to accomplish this on her own. "Go ahead. Finish. I'll be along."

But then Harper recalled the fire chief's speech. The one about "teamwork" and "partnerships" and she hunkered down in the mud beside the man she definitely wanted by her side for the rest of her life.

Take me. Be mine.

"I'll wait right here for you," she told him. Because while she wasn't quite strong enough to pick him up, she'd always be there for him if he fell.

That was the real change that had happened to her in Eagle's Ridge, she realized now. She'd gained confidence in herself to know that she could be a protector, defender, and partner to Zane too. Stroking his back with muddy fingers, she felt a new thrilling sort of serenity course through her bloodstream—a kind of lover's high, she thought.

It didn't take long for Zane to regain his breath and she helped him to his feet. They looked at each other and exchanged smiles. Then, filthy and exhausted, they limped toward the finish and stepped over the line, hand-in-hand.

Together.

Nearby, another volunteer was stationed with a hose to wash down the finishers. They waited their turn, fingers still entwined, while Zane's people gathered around them, including Adam, Jane, Brenda, Sam, Wyatt, and Bailey.

"I'm so sorry I lost control of Gambler," his sister said. "We've got another item to put on the Terror List."

Ryder strolled up with the dog then, now back under control. He had the megaphone in his other hand.

"Confiscated," he said, holding it up. "I'm not taking any chances. And this dog needs to be enrolled in obedience school immediately."

The hose person beckoned them forward. Harper tried to disentangle their hands, but Zane said, "I'm not taking any chances either," and they stood together under the spray as layers of mud slid away.

Only then, when they were dripping, but clean, did Harper realize what he was wearing over his athletic shorts and T-shirt.

A red, blue, and gold spangled costume, complete with skirt, bodice, arm bands, and head ornament.

She stared. "What's this?" Her free hand gestured toward him.

Zane sighed. "The outcome of a little bet." He shot a fulminating look at Wyatt. "You better be ready to pack your bags and include a big ol' shovel, friend, if the lady won't accept that I'm in love with her and says she feels the same."

Everyone surrounding them appeared to be caught somewhere between laughter and concern.

But she shut them out and looked only at the man who'd made a very public declaration in a town that would talk about this for years to come.

While dressed as Wonder Woman, in fact.

"You do love me," she said, amazed all over again, but now believing it completely.

"Enough to don this ridiculous costume," he said promptly. Then he grinned. "Remind me to outfit that John Westbrook statue in something more macho next time."

"What?"

"Never mind." He pulled her into his arms, either no longer patient, very sure of her, or some of both. "Tell me you're in love with me too," he demanded.

"I'm in love with you too." Why not say it? She was brave enough to take the chance now. The chance to have it all.

"We're setting a date," he said firmly. "A wedding date. Today. Tonight. Soonest."

Her eyes rounded.

"Because a person once told me that a man who wants to marry someone should want to settle on a date right away."

He'd always heard her, hadn't he?

"Okay." Harper thought she might float off the

ground, she felt that light. Her hands gripped Wonder Woman's now-tattered bodice as she looked into the handsome, beloved face of Zane Tucker. Only her guy could look so sexy and not an iota less manly wearing a superheroine's tiara. "Bet me we'll be happy?"

"I'll take that bet." He kissed her. "And we'll both end up winners."

THE END

Get the complete series:

Ryder – Barbara Freethy (#1)
Adam – Roxanne St. Claire (#2)
Zane – Christie Ridgway (#3)
Wyatt – Lynn Raye Harris (#4)
Jack – Julia London (#5)
Noah – Cristin Harber (#6)
Ford – Samantha Chase (#7)

About The Author

Christie Ridgway is the author of over fifty novels of contemporary romance. All her books are both sexy and emotional and tell about heroes and heroines who learn to believe in the power of love. A *USA Today* bestseller, Christie is a six-time RITA finalist and has won best contemporary romance of the year and career achievement awards from *Romantic Times Book Reviews*.

A native of California, Christie now resides in the southern part of the state with her family. Inspired by the beaches, mountains, and cities that surround her, she writes tales of sunny days and steamy nights. For a complete list of books, excerpts, and news on the latest going on with Christie:

Visit Christie's Website:
www. christieridgway.net

Join Christie on Facebook:
www.facebook.com/christieridgway

Follow Christie on Twitter:
http://www.twitter.com/christieridgway

Made in the USA
Monee, IL
28 December 2019

19596640R00136